A Home Subscription! It's the easiest and most convenient way to get every one of the exciting Coventry Romance Novels! ...And you get 4 of them FREE!

You pay nothing extra for this convenience: there are no additional charges...you don't even pay for postage! Fill out and send us the handy coupon now, and we'll send you 4 exciting Coventry Romance novels absolutely FREE!

SEND NO MONEY, GET THESE
FOUR BOOKS FREE!

▬▬ ▬▬ ▬▬ ▬▬ ▬▬ ▬▬ ▬▬ ▬▬ ▬▬ ▬▬

C0781

MAIL THIS COUPON TODAY TO:
COVENTRY HOME
SUBSCRIPTION SERVICE
6 COMMERCIAL STREET
HICKSVILLE, NEW YORK 11801

YES, please start a Coventry Romance Home Subscription in my name, and send me FREE and without obligation to buy, my 4 Coventry Romances. If you do not hear from me after I have examined my 4 FREE books, please send me the 6 new Coventry Romances each month as soon as they come off the presses. I understand that I will be billed only $11.70 for all 6 books. There are no shipping and handling nor any other hidden charges. There is no minimum number of monthly purchases that I have to make. In fact, I can cancel my subscription at any time. The first 4 FREE books are mine to keep as a gift, even if I do not buy any additional books.

For added convenience, your monthly subscription may be charged automatically to your credit card.

☐ Master Charge   ☐ Visa
    42101   **42101**

Credit Card # _____

Expiration Date _____

Name _____
                      Please Print

Address _____

City _____ State _____ Zip _____

Signature _____

☐ Bill Me Direct Each Month **40105**

This offer expires Dec. 31, 1981. Prices subject to change without notice. Publisher reserves the right to substitute alternate FREE books. Sales tax collected where required by law. Offer valid for new members only.

A MARRIAGE ARRANGED

a novel by

Mira Stables

FAWCETT COVENTRY • NEW YORK

A MARRIAGE ARRANGED

This book contains the complete text of the original hardcover edition.

Published by Fawcett Coventry Books, a unit of CBS Publications, the Consumer Publishing Division of CBS Inc., by arrangement with Robert Hale Limited

ISBN: 0-449-50192-2

Printed in the United States of America

First Fawcett Coventry printing: July 1981

10   9   8   7   6   5   4   3   2   1

A MARRIAGE
ARRANGED

One

It was a stranger who opened the gates to him; those gates which he remembered as standing always hospitably open. Briefly he wondered what had happened to Mrs. Beechey who had so often regaled a band of hungry little marauders with jam tarts and lemonade. Perhaps at a more convenient time he could enquire. Meanwhile he dropped a coin into a ready palm and rode on up to the house.

He did not hurry. His appointment was not until eleven o'clock and he was early. To arrive before his time might give an impression of eagerness that he would prefer to avoid. He let Warlock drop to a walk and yielded to an unwontedly sentimental mood as familiar surroundings recalled the days of his childhood.

It had been a happy one. He had been seven when his father had succeeded unexpectedly to the Wellasford estates. Julian had not been concerned with this sudden elevation to the ranks of the nobility, but to a boy brought up in the shabby-genteel lodgings that fell to the lot of a soldier who was almost wholly dependent on his pay, Wellasford was a paradise. He saw very little of his father, even though that gentleman had sold out of the army when he inherited the title. Papa spent a good deal of his time in Town, which was easy of access—no more than two hours if conditions were good. Julian could remember hearing him say that it was fortunate that Wellasford was situated in Hertfordshire, though Sussex would have been even better. He could remember, too, that he had been furious at this patronising speech, since to him Wellasford was already perfect.

On the whole he had been glad that Papa was away so much. Mama, small gentle Mama, had seen to it that he had companions a-plenty with whom to share his new kingdom. Between the Rectory children and a whole brood of Merridews—from Caroline, a year older than himself and very *managing* to Johnnie, a plump and placid four-year-old—he scarcely realised that he was an only child. Hugh—the Rector's elder boy—was a demi-god of twelve, invested with all the glamour of the schoolboy. Between him and Johnnie Merridew, Julian grew up as a very ordinary healthy little ragamuffin, learning to take the occasional hard knock and to be tolerant, even at times generous, towards his weaker brethren. The children had filled the places of brothers and sisters—yet he had almost entirely lost track of them. Hugh had joined the army and had lost a leg at Breed's Hill. Caro had married—and at seventeen he had thought himself heart-broken for at least a week. He doubted now if he would recognise her if they should chance to meet.

Rounding the bend in the avenue he caught a distant glimpse of the stretch of level turf where they had raced their ponies. There was the old elm which had cost him a broken leg when Hugh had dared him to climb it. And here was the terrace where Mama had told him countless stories and played every imaginable kind of game with him in an attempt to beguile the tedium of convalescence, while he gave her about half his attention and fidgeted and fumed to be off with the others. Darling Mama! What a horrid little beast he had been. He had never truly valued her until she had died, quite suddenly, while he was away at school. But he would never forget the utter desolation of the long summer holiday that had come shortly after his bereavement. If he had thought to find a closer companionship with his father in their mutual loss, the hope was soon abandoned. Papa had scant patience with an awkward, diffident sixteen-year-old. Julian's stumbling attempts to help with the running of Wellasford were rejected. And since, in fact, he knew a great deal more about good husbandry than did Papa, who was concerned only to wring the last shilling out of estates already impoverished by years of mismanagement, he soon abandoned them in despair. Growing up in the place, counting the tenants as his friends, he understood something of its needs. But talking to Papa was useless.

It was a rift that was destined to widen. As Julian grew older and his father's anxiety over debts and mortgages increased, the older man came to resent his son's timid suggestions more and more bitterly. When the boy begged to be allowed to leave school and devote himself to salvaging what remained, he was curtly informed that he was destined for the army, as were all male Wellasfords. At present, said his father, with bitter emphasis, the welfare of the estate was not his concern. Indeed, it was the speaker's profound hope that it would be many years before *that* interesting situation arose.

After so crushing a repulse there was nothing more to be said. Lord Wellasford, growing a little more amiable as the level in the burgundy bottle sank, was at some pains to explain to his heir that he had no intention of allowing him to sink to the level of a country bumpkin. Sooner or later the luck must turn. For a man whom fortune favoured there was money enough to be made without the toil and muck of farming. He had enjoyed a splendid run of luck at Boodles only a month past. It was a pity that the horse on which he had staked this gift-gold had been unplaced. But he regarded this as a minor set-back—just Lady Luck's way of testing his faith in her. Only let Julian have patience and he would see how well things would turn out. Meanwhile he could pursue a military career and see something of the world. The boy, regarding his slightly tipsy sire with desperate eyes, assented numbly. But, decided this much older Julian, that was probably when the dream was born. Dream—or obsession. Some day, somehow, he would be master of Wellasford. And he would serve and cherish it as it deserved.

He surveyed it now, turning the last bend in the avenue with the house coming into sight. No cold Palladian mansion, but a house that had grown with the centuries from the humble manor of the early years to spread wings in the reign of Queen Anne. There it lay—gracious, warm, welcoming. *Exactly* as he remembered it, he thought, forgetting its old-time shabbiness, ignoring its present air of well-being. A new surge of resolution filled him. Whatever the price, he must make it his.

He had accepted velvet-smooth lawns and well-kept borders without a thought, but it was impossible to overlook the transformation of the great hall, and of the library into which he was presently ushered. A few things remained from the past, mostly items of some antiquity—a display of ancient weapons—a suit of armour—a number of portraits of long-dead Wellasfords. The hotch-potch of slightly battered furniture that he remembered with affection had been swept away entirely. Here was dignity, craftsmanship of the highest order, serene comfort. There was nothing to strike a false note or to jar on the most sensitive taste. If he had not known the truth he would have assumed quite naturally that these furnishings had grown old with the house. Yet skilfully as it had been done, he found himself resenting the change, and it was with some stiffness that he acknowledged his host's polite greeting.

Mr. Nathaniel Morley had not achieved the age of eight and forty nor turned a comfortable inheritance into the kind of fortune that made him a power in the land without acquiring the ability to sum up a man and his reactions with a fair degree of accuracy.

"I expect you find the place a good deal changed," he suggested, when he had seated his guest in a beautiful oak and leather chair that might have been young when Cromwell was a boy. "Unfortunately it had become very necessary. Your father was rarely in residence here during his latter years, and after old Blackburn died there was no one to take order for regular maintenance and repairs. Old buildings fall into decay very quickly under such circumstances. I have tried to restore and replace as much as possible, and at least to ensure that what is necessarily new should harmonise with the original fabric. I trust that, upon more leisurely inspection, you will feel that I have achieved a tolerable compromise."

Lord Wellasford responded with a slight bow and a hint of a smile, but his pose did not relax. "You are very good, sir. But I have already seen enough to realise that your taste is impeccable." And then, his natural honesty evoking the reluctant tribute, "I have never seen the house look so well. But I will not pretend to wholehearted satisfaction in the sight, any more than I will waste your valuable time on an inspection that would only fill me with bitter envy. The fact is, sir, that it was not just idle curiosity that prompted me to request this interview, nor even a sentimental wish to re-visit my childhood home. It is my earnest desire to persuade you to sell it back to me, and it is plain from the care that has gone into its restoration—I might almost say its resuscitation," he corrected wryly—"that my mission is not like to prove an easy one."

Mr. Morley regarded him gravely, though there was a hint of humour about the set of his rather severe mouth. "Edgewick warned me that you preferred the straightforward approach," he said thoughtfully. "Your military training, I apprehend."

His lordship shrugged. "Perhaps. I believe

it is thought to leave an indelible mark. Though it is close on three years since I sold out and since then I have been engaged in business dealings in India. Where the direct approach is useless."

There was a hint of surprise in Mr. Morley's face. "That I well believe, having myself had extensive dealings in Eastern countries. But I very much regret, milord—Edgewick should have warned you—that I have no intention of selling."

"So he did, sir. But I could not be satisfied until I had talked to you myself. I am well aware that you are a busy man and that your time is valuable." He hesitated there for a moment. He had meant to say that he was very willing to pay for that time, but something about the presence of the man who confronted him sounded a warning. Mr Morley might spring from the merchant classes, might have attained his present affluence solely by his own financial genius, but there was something about his easy bearing, his unassuming manners that commanded respect. He was not a man who would take kindly to patronage.

Julian said, "I could not rest until I felt that I fully understood the circumstances that brought Wellasford into your possession. And, indeed, that *you* understood my position. You may say it is no concern of mine, which is true. I can only crave your indulgence."

He had not meant to plead, intending rather a dignified and business-like approach backed by a handsome offer. But instinct had served him well. Mr. Morley reacted to the note of painful bewilderment in the deep pleasant voice.

"If it is clearly understood that under no circumstances am I prepared to sell, I am quite willing to answer any questions that you choose to ask," he suggested.

"Thank you, sir. At least then I shall know where I stand. I was, of course, already aware that the estate was not entailed. But it has been in the same family since the reign of James the First. My father was only a distant cousin, but surely he must have had *some* family feeling. A second mortgage, yes, if he was hard pressed. But what in heaven's name persuaded him to sell outright? To make it impossible for me to redeem it, which was always my intention."

Mr. Morley considered his reply carefully. "You should not blame your father too severely, milord," he said quietly. "The estate was already grossly encumbered when he succeeded, and his personal fortune, I was given to understand, was not large. Also, unfortunately, he was an incurable gamester, with all the optimism that seems to be peculiar to gentlemen of that persuasion. He was not attracted to the life of the country squire, living quietly and economically, taking his pleasure in fruitful acres. He once said to me—we became fairly intimate after I bought the Merridew place—that until he inherited Wellasford his whole life had been penny-pinching and putting a bold face on nothing. Wellasford at least allowed him to live the life of a gentleman of means. And, alas, to bet beyond them. But on that head I must say no more." He looked slightly discomfited as though he had already said too much, but presently went on, "As for second mortgages, milord, these you must know are very expensive, carrying a high rate of interest. Also in this case there would have been difficulties, the security not very satisfactory—the house neglected, the land in bad heart."

He paused briefly in response to the slight jerk of Julian's chin, but it was better to have done with the sorry tale. "As for redeeming the mortgages—I am sorry for it, but you said you wanted to know how you stood. He never forgave you for selling out of the army. You did so, I believe, in '82, when you inherited Sir Thomas Loring's fortune."

"My godfather," assented Julian. "My mother's brother. But why should that set him against me?"

Mr. Morley shrugged. "How can one say? Perhaps he felt that you had it in your power to have relieved him of certain minor irritants. I was not his only creditor, you know. But if it is any comfort to you, it was already too late to save the Wellasford estates. Those had been in my possession for a year and more, though it was part of the bargain that his tenancy should last for the term of his life."

Julian choked back bitter words. His father had assured his own comfort without loss of consequence and left nothing but debts for his son. *That* he could have forgiven. But to have tossed away all chance of that son's redeeming the place without even consulting him was beyond pardon.

He said slowly, "Even if I had come home immediately he would not have listened to me. He never did so. Resented any interest I showed in the place. Nor would I have been willing to frank him in his gaming excesses. But my uncle's fortune derived mainly from business interests in India and it was necessary for me to go out there to look into their organisation."

Mr. Morley looked at him curiously. This was unexpected. "Did you find it an interesting experience?" he probed gently.

"I did indeed," returned Julian, thankful for a brief respite from the painful topic of his father's misdoings. "I was more ignorant than any raw recruit, but my uncle must have been a good judge of men. He had chosen his managers admirably. They were very patient with me. If I had not been summoned home by my father's death it would have been difficult to tear myself away. I was just beginning to get a grasp of the way things are run out there. Very different from English methods—and I found it fascinating. Much more to my taste than army life," he added with a rueful twinkle.

There was more to this young man than to most of his class, decided his host. It made no difference, of course, as regards Wellasford. But since he had given up a morning to this interview he might as well get some enjoyment out of it. He had always found the study of his fellow men of absorbing interest, and a scion of the aristocracy who openly proclaimed that he found business methods more to his liking than army life was certainly a rare specimen.

"You did not enjoy your military life?" he said enquiringly.

"Oh—it was perfectly tolerable for the most part," shrugged Julian. "I expect the fault was in myself. I was not an enthusiast. I did no more than was necesary to keep out of trouble and to do what was required of me. I managed well enough until the American war. Think me a renegade if you will, though I never failed in my duties and did not sell out until hostilities ended, but *that* turned my stomach. The fellows we were fighting might have been our brothers or cousins. In some cases they were. And I had never cherished military ambitions. The army career was my father's notion. Though I daresay I'd fight as willingly as the next if the safety of Wellasford was at stake," he ended with a rueful grimace.

Mr. Morley nodded thoughtfully. "I am sorry for your disappointment," he said quietly, "but I would not have you delude yourself with false hopes. No persuasions you could use, no price that you might offer would induce me to sell. Since you have been so open and honest, I will admit in my turn that it has been my fixed purpose to buy Wellasford for more than twenty years, and that your father's reckless folly played into my hands. Don't misunderstand me. I neither encouraged him to gamble beyond his means nor cheated him over the price. You may examine all the documents relating to the various transactions with my very good will. But I *did* make it my business to be always on hand when I knew him to be particularly hard pressed and to be a model of discretion with regard to our dealings. I doubt if any of his friends guessed the true state of affairs."

Despite his bitter disappointment, Julian was aware of some degree of curiosity. "I find your attitude surprising, sir," he said bluntly. "Why Wellasford? There must be at least a dozen estates within easy reach of Town that might have served your purpose just as well. Though I hold the place in deep affection I am willing to admit that it is not particularly imposing. It never found fame in the history books, won only the briefest mention in Cary's Survey—and it will be years before you get anything like a decent return on the capital that you must have poured into it. Could you not have found some other place more worthy of your time and attention?"

Mr. Morley shook his head. "No. I will not

enter into my reasons, except to say that they were purely personal and had nothing whatever to do with either your father or yourself. May we now regard the matter as closed?"

Impossible to persist. As it was he had been shown a tolerance and courtesy beyond what might reasonably have been expected. Rather guiltily he accepted his host's offer of refreshment and allowed himself to be drawn into conversation upon topics of general interest.

He found Mr. Morley well-informed—which he had expected—and entertaining—which he had not. He was witty, mildly cynical, and had a knack of describing some of the country's more inept politicians in one or two devastating phrases that stripped them of pomposity and self-consequence and exposed them for the bumbling incompetents that they had shown themselves in their conduct of the late war. He spoke with deep concern of the steady deterioration of affairs in France. Finally, as he replenished their glasses, he enquired with some diffidence as to Julian's future plans. Did he think of going back to India?

"Not immediately. My uncle left me his home, Pittsfield House in Surrey. Near Caterham. It is not very large, but there are three farms. I must make the acquaintance of my tenants and ensure that all is well with them before I make further plans."

Mr. Morley nodded. "There I envy you," he said simply. "Growing up as you did, it comes naturally to you. I make no doubt your tenants will confide in you without loss of time. No doubt they will try you out at first to discover if you're a green 'un—an easy touch as I would phrase it. But once they have decided that you are awake to the time of day, your troubles will be over. It is a relationship of slow growth, like most things in country living, and can never be acquired late in life. You say I have made a success of Wellasford. The house—perhaps. But as regards the land I am a mere cypher. The tenants are polite—and completely remote, as only your English rustic knows how. I am obliged to employ a bailiff; to content myself with dutiful curtseys and pulling of forelocks; and I shall never bridge the gap between us; never know if they are content and well cared for, or if my bailiff is cheating me wholesale and causing them to suffer hardship in the process."

There was a note of sincere regret in the half-laughing complaint. Moreover it was one that Julian perfectly understood, and it won his sympathy, even though at the same time he was aware of a certain degree of satisfaction that some part of Wellasford still clung to the old loyalties. He reconciled these conflicting feelings as best he could, agreeing that country folk could be remarkably cross-grained and enquiring after various old acquaintances who came into this category and after Mrs. Beechey who did not. The answers were in general satisfactory though, as was only to be expected, time had left certain gaps in the community.

"I don't suppose you'd care to ride over to Little Wittans with me," suggested Mr. Morley tentatively. "Young Thorpe is one of your awkward customers. You'll remember his father—as decent a fellow as you'd meet in a month of Sundays. The boy went off to America to seek his fortune. Seems he didn't find it—and been blue as megrim ever since he came back. Edgewick advised me against letting him take the place over, but there was his mother to think about as well, and I didn't care for the notion of turning her out. He'll be about your age—Thorpe. Maybe a word with you would cheer him up. Certainly old Mrs. Thorpe would be both pleased and proud to welcome you."

Put like that it was difficult to refuse, especially as he had no other engagement to

plead as excuse. "Just comfortable time before dinner," announced Mr. Morley cheerfully. "You'll take pot-luck with us, won't
you?" And seeing Julian's surprised face and
swift glance at the mantel clock, added, "I
dine at three, after the fashion of my boy-
hood. You will be accustomed to keeping fashionable hours, but I daresay you'll be pretty
sharp-set by the time we've ridden to Little
Wittans and back."

To decline an invitation so phrased must
be both hurtful and ill-bred. Julian, who could
perfectly well administer a crushing snub
when he felt it to be necessary, smiled pleasantly and thanked his host.

Two

The ride was surprisingly pleasant. Despite
his advancing years Mr. Morley proved to be
an accomplished horseman. Julian had reckoned as much at first sight of the good-
looking bay that was led out for his use. He
swung into the saddle without the aid of
groom or mounting block and his neat, spare
figure moulded itself to his mount's easy action so that horse and man seemed to be one.
The negligent ease with which he controlled
the powerful animal was impressive, and when
they let the horses out on a tempting stretch
of turf, Julian was hard put to it to keep up
with the flying bay.

The visit to Little Wittans proved abortive. It went smoothly enough, though Julian was considerably embarrassed by old Mrs. Thorpe's insistence on referring to him as the young master. But her son was not at home, having taken some young calves to market, and she doubted he would not be back before milking time. One could not help noticing that the farm and its buildings were in an excellent state of repair and that, so far as a cursory survey went, both crops and stock were flourishing. A good landlord made for good farming, thought Julian bitterly, remembering the tumbledown state of some of the buildings in his father's day. The tenants, at any rate, had benefited by the change of ownership.

But such reflections were futile. He drained the tankard of home-brewed ale that Mrs. Thorpe had insisted that they try, expressed the hope that it had not made him so top heavy that he would fall off Warlock, and bade his hostess farewell, gently evading her eager suggestions that the gentlemen should ride over again when Will was at home. "Which he mostly always is, your honour, 'cept just sometimes on market days."

They trotted off briskly, Mr. Morley explaining that he had made something of a fetish of punctuality and did not care to be late for meals. "No use training your servants with such pains and then setting them a bad example," he remarked sensibly, and allowed the bay to break into a canter.

It was strange and a little odd to sit down to a meal at Wellasford as a guest. Fortunately Mr. Morley did not use the family dining room, explaining that he preferred the small breakfast parlour with its view across the rose garden to the trees of the park. "Except when we are a large party," he added, "which is rarely. My daughter shares my liking for a quiet going on."

Julian felt a faint stir of surprise. He was almost sure that the lawyer had described Mr. Morley as a bachelor. Or perhaps he had just said that there was no son to inherit the estate. Yes, that was it. Julian could remember the very dubious expression with which Mr. Edgewick had conceded that this *might* be a deciding factor when trying to persuade Mr. Morley to sell. Well—*that* dream was over. There was no question of selling. And if there was no son to inherit, it seemed that there was a daughter. No mention of a wife, though. Perhaps Mr. Morley was a widower. He wished that he was a little better informed about his host's circumstances. One could blunder badly through ignorance. A swift sidelong glance showed him that the dinner table was laid for three. Presumably Miss Morley would join them for dinner.

Even as the thought crossed his mind, Mr. Morley said smilingly, "I trust that Anna will not keep us waiting, after all my talk about punctuality. I daresay she is changing her dress."

On the last word an expression of almost ludicrous dismay crossed his countenance. "Dress!" he repeated feebly. "I forgot to warn her! Well, indeed, I did not really know, did I? That you would be dining with us, I mean."

He looked so shattered, so different from the brisk and competent man of affairs, that Julian felt quite sorry for him. He was on the brink of suggesting that he should make a hasty departure and *not,* after all, stay to dinner, though to speak truth he now very much wanted to stay. Not only because he was, as Mr. Morley had prophesied, exceedingly hungry, but because his curiosity had been aroused by that gentleman's obvious agitation. But it was already too late. The door opened gently and a girl came into the room.

For a moment Julian forgot all about the behaviour proper to a gentleman in the presence of a young lady who was also, he supposed, his hostess. His mouth dropped open and he frankly gaped. If he had *had* any coherent thoughts about the girl's appearance, he would have concluded that she had come down to dinner in her dressing gown. It was a loose, flowing garment in a rather charming shade of green, with huge sleeves that hung in points to the floor. Hair that was dressed in two thick plaits accentuated the dressing gown effect, save that the ends of the plaits were bound with some kind of filigree work of gold, set with sparkling coloured stones. The green gown had a plain round neckline, and a heavy gold necklace, beautifully worked and obviously of great antiquity, circled the base of the girl's throat and gave Julian the clue to the mystery. Mr. Morley's passion for the ancient and the beautiful, so plainly to be seen in his restoration of Wellasford, had been extended to guide his daughter's choice of costume.

For a moment the lady was the most composed of the three. She had coloured to the roots of her hair at the realisation that there was a stranger in the room, but she betrayed no other sign of embarrassment or nervousness, coming forward placidly while her father struggled with a medley of apologetic and explanatory phrases and Julian pulled himself together and executed his best bow. She appeared to follow her father's disjointed account without difficulty, and only said quietly, "It is a pity that I was not forewarned. I would have ordered one or two side dishes. Now, I fear, it will indeed be pot-luck. But you must blame Papa, sir, who is so much put about by his neglect that he has not even remembered to tell me your name."

This prosaic approach exerted a powerfully calming effect on Mr. Morley. He sighed in a relieved sort of way and presented Lord Wellasford to his daughter Anastasia in due form.

The dinner was indeed a good deal simpler than the meals that were customarily served in more elevated circles. The first course consisted of rump of beef with dumplings, a roast fowl and cod with oyster sauce. This was removed with a boiled tongue, an apple pie, a dish of curd cakes and a bowl of fresh fruit. There were no elaborate garnishes, but in marked contrast with many more elegant dinners the food was beautifully cooked and the hot dishes were piping hot. Much to the gratification of his host, Julian did ample justice to this good plain fare. The gentlemen enjoyed an excellent claret, but a jug of rich creamy milk was set before Miss Morley, and

32

her father drew her attention to this once or twice, adjuring her to drink it all up. She obeyed him, but Julian thought she did not relish it over much. And small wonder. The girl must be four or five and twenty, surely too old for such nursery treatment. He noticed, casually, that she partook very sparingly of such dishes as she selected and declined pie and cake in favour of a peach. She also declined his own offer to prepare this fruit for her, biting into it with relish so that the juice ran down her chin.

This minor contretemps did not distress her. She grinned impishly at her father who was inclined to draw a solemn mouth over her hoydenish tricks, and told him that half the flavour of the fruit was lost in the careful preparation. Julian promptly took issue with her on this head, rather meanly quoting the pineapple as a prime example of the opposite view. This she was obliged to concede, but made a prompt recover by asking him demurely how often he ate pineapple, and whether he did not think that a good English *apple*, in its prime, was best eaten as God had intended when he gave man hands and teeth.

This frivolous interlude did much to lighten the rather solemn atmosphere in which they had begun the meal. It proceeded in leisurely

fashion, Miss Morley negligently eating grapes
while the men-folk attended to the more solid
viands and cracked a second bottle of claret.
Talk ran merrily on a number of subjects,
although Miss Morley's unusual choice of
costume was not one of them. Julian found
her perfectly conversable. She had a well-
informed mind and contributed her share
towards the various exchanges, though she
left the initiation of new topics to the gentlemen. She was not the kind of female who
appealed to him—too plump for his taste and
seemingly devoid of feminine artifice. He preferred something kittenish and coy. But he
thought her manners very pleasing—frank
without being forward—and he admired the
quiet dignity with which she had carried
off the awkward situation created by her peculiar costume. As a matter of fact it was
quite an attractive sort of costume in its way,
the colour ideally chosen to set off the wearer's
fair skin and those great ropes of golden hair.
He tried to visualise her dressed in the cur-
rent mode but found it difficult since her
loose draperies concealed her figure and he
could not imagine how such a quantity of
hair could be arranged in a fashionable style,
so he abandoned idle speculation and turned
his attention to his host who was asking his

views on the merits of claret as opposed to the heavier burgundy which was more universally popular.

He did not notice that Mr. Morley was gradually withdrawing from the talk, occasionally tossing in some comment or question that set the ball rolling again, and then studying the animated faces of his table companions with a very thoughtful air. It was he who skilfully turned the talk to Julian's recent experiences in India. The young man's own vivid interest was infectious. He talked easily and well, and Miss Morley's rather heavy countenance glowed into something approaching beauty as she poured out her eager questions.

Presently Mr. Morley broke across a slight pause in the recital to say gently, "If you will excuse us, my dear, there are one or two matters that I would like to discuss with his lordship before he leaves us. And though the moon is at the full, the roads are none too safe after dark. Footpads and highwaymen have been pretty active of late, their numbers augmented by the scaff and raff of the army who have no gainful occupation now that the war is over."

The girl rose immediately, her brief vivacity dying, her face composed in an expression of decorous courtesy. "Yes, indeed," she said. "I have been very remiss. Pray forgive me, milord, and permit me to thank you for a most enjoyable talk. I wish you a safe journey." She curtsied formally and withdrew with dignity, her long skirts sweeping behind her as Julian sprang to open the door.

He found himself quite indignant on her behalf. Her father seemed to treat her as something between a doll to be dressed for his pleasure—for surely the girl herself had never evolved that peculiar rig—and a child scarcely out of the nursery. But after all it was no bread and butter of his and he was unlikely to visit Wellasford again. He resumed his seat, declined a suggestion of port or madeira to round off his dinner but accepted another glass of claret and waited politely to hear what his host had to say.

That gentleman did not hesitate. "First I would like to explain about Anna's dress," he said simply. "I would not have you think her an eccentric. As I daresay you have realised, anything of beauty and antiquity holds a deep fascination for me. I don't know if you noticed the necklace she was wearing. It is Roman work and dates back to the second century. But to be brief, I have devoted much of my leisure to collecting jewellery, china, silver and gold ornaments, most of them designed centuries ago. But many things are perishable. Unless it has been very carefully kept, any kind of fabric is likely to crumble at a touch. So where dress is concerned I have had originals that appealed to me accurately copied and Anna humours me by wearing them when we dine alone. I was sadly at fault in not warning her that tonight we would *not* be alone, and in exposing her to possible discomfort. I owe you thanks for treating the matter as the merest commonplace and for setting the poor child at her ease."

"Well as to that, sir, it is your daughter herself who deserves your thanks. I confess that her appearance *was* something of a surprise. But her dignity of bearing, her complete absence of self-consciousness made acceptance both easy and natural."

Mr. Morley looked pleased. "I thought you were hitting it off very comfortably together," he observed. "Anna does not go into Society enough. My fault, I fear. We go on so contentedly that I do not urge her to a life that would deprive me of her company. She *did* have a Season in Town when she was eighteen. My sister took her to a great many parties and showed her all the sights, but by what I could make out the child didn't care for it above half. Certainly she seemed thankful enough to come home. And since then I have been a good deal occupied, partly with business affairs, partly with"—he hesitated briefly, then plunged boldly on—"with my arrangements to take over Wellasford. The question of Anna's future did not seem particularly urgent. Indeed it was only tonight, seeing her so self-possessed in a dilemma of *my* making, that I realised how fast she is growing up."

Julian would have said that she was definitely grown up, though he could not see that it was any concern of his. He assumed an expression of polite interest and sipped his claret.

Mr. Morley fell silent for a moment, then raised his head suddenly and jerked out, "I said I would never sell Wellasford, and I hold by that. At my death it will go to Anna, who is my sole heir. Watching the two of you tonight, so pleasant and affable together, the thought came into my head—how if you was to marry? No!" as Julian choked on his wine, his whole attitude indicative of protest, "Hear me out if you please. It was only a thought. You are free to do as you wish and nothing would persuade me to put pressure on Anna. But there could be no harm in the two of you becoming better acquainted. You *might* decide that you were pretty well suited after all. And if you did, well—that would bring Wellasford back to you and give Anna a husband that I've taken quite a liking to. In the general way I'll admit that I've some prejudice against your sort, and good reason for it, but you strike me as being rather out of the common run. Not above being civil and pleasant despite your disappointment over Wellasford, and a shrewd head on your shoulders unless I'm sorely mistaken, which isn't likely. Too short acquaintance to be sure of anything else, but you might make my Anna a good husband if you gave your mind to it, though I'll allow that it's not for me to decide. All I'm asking is that you should think it over for a bit, because if you should fall in with my views there's one or two things that it's only right you should know."

He lapsed into silence once more, occupying himself with replenishing their glasses.

Julian was not so much thoughtful as slightly dazed by the bombshell which had burst upon him without warning. His first reaction had been to repudiate the whole idea in terms which would certainly have put an end to any hope of further cordial relations with his host. But Mr. Morley had been wise when he insisted that his guest take time to think things over. Was it so outrageous after all? Certainly not in its initial stages. He was only being asked to improve his acquaintance with Miss Morley in order to give the pair of them an opportunity of discovering whether a marriage between them might prove agreeable to both. Put in that way it was no more than fair business dealing. He could offer a title, the old house in Surrey and a comfortable fortune. Miss Morley could give him back Wellasford. *That* temptation was a strong one. He had been willing to pay a high price for his old home. Was this price too high?

But no need to think of that yet. There could be no harm in extending his knowledge of Miss Morley's disposition, her tastes and preferences, always ensuring that *she* understood the terms of the suggested bargain as clearly as he did. He had no intention of arousing hopes of romance in a maiden heart that he suspected of being extremely unsophisticated, despite the lady's age and that one Season in Town. If that was understood—

These views he presently explained to Mr. Morley, a little hesitant at first, waxing insistent when Mr. Morley was inclined to demur about explaining the situation to the lady. Only on that understanding, he said firmly, was he prepared to go any further with the business, which, he admitted, might well be successful if given a fair chance. Mr. Morley eventually capitulated, though not without one final fling.

"Your scruples, milord, give me an excellent notion of your honesty in business dealings. I doubt, though, if you have much knowledge of the opposite sex or the best way to handle them."

Julian grinned. "That should count in my favour, surely? I confess that I have no more experience of females than one milk and water romance when I was a mere schoolboy, and the casual adventures that are the common lot of the military man. I have never met the girl with whom I wished to share the rest of my life."

Mr. Morley nodded thoughtfully. "I would suggest, then, that you go back to Town and make arrangements to remove to Wellasford for a month or so, as soon as may be convenient. At such close quarters that should be long enough to ascertain your feelings for each other."

Julian nodded. "Ample time. I have one or two matters to settle while I am in Town but

I would expect to be with you in a week's time."

There was a heavy pause. Quite suddenly Mr. Morley looked ages older. In a voice utterly devoid of emotion he said, "First there is one thing that I must explain. When that is done you are perfectly free to withdraw from the bargain and I shall not hold it against you. But it is best done now. Like you, I prefer to see my way clear. Small use in forging ahead, only to meet an insuperable obstacle just when things are in a promising way."

Julian met his gaze steadily, aware of an odd feeling of pity for which there was no reasonable cause. The heavy-lidded grey eyes that were reproduced in his daughter were full of pain, but he lifted his head gallantly enough as he said, "I am unmarried. Anastasia is my adopted daughter—legally adopted. She is my younger sister's child; and she was born out of wedlock."

The shock was severe, there could be no denying. The Wellasfords had been proud—though there was little enough to be proud of today, reminded Julian's sense of fair play. But it was instinctive pity for the dumb suffering in the haggard face that prompted him to say gently, "And her father?"

There was a faint relaxation in the taut pose. "His blood was as good as yours. He was a soldier, and died on the field of battle. Whether, if he had lived, he would have married my sister, I cannot say. *She* thought so. But women are easily cozened with fair promises. I told you I had good cause to dislike your kind. At least now you know why."

Julian did not understand what prompted his answer. Surely he was not actuated by pity—not even by mild sympathy—for the man who had filched Wellasford! Filched it, too, by means which might be strictly legal but were certainly not above criticism. Perhaps, partly, it was the subtle flattery of not being specifically asked to respect the confidence reposed in him, partly regret for the bringing down of that gallant façade. For certainly his host—the owner of beloved Wellasford—was at his mercy.

He said gently, "I am honoured by your confidence, sir. I should think I could clear up my outstanding commitment by next Thursday. Would that be convenient for you?"

Three

He set out for Wellasford a week later in less obliging mood, having spent much of the intervening time in wondering how he had been persuaded to subscribe to such a madbrained scheme. He had thought seriously of writing to Mr. Morley to say that he had changed his mind. Better to withdraw now and save all parties a deal of embarrassment.

Next day he would find himself wondering if the suggested marriage was really so ridiculous, so impossible. Arranged marriages were a commonplace in his class of society. Had his father pursued the normal pattern it was very likely that some such match would have been arranged for Julian. A well-born maiden, comfortably dowered and well-trained in the duties of wifehood—including that of closing her eyes to such of her husband's extra-marital adventures as chanced to come to her notice. She herself, of course, would not be permitted such licence until she had produced an heir, and even then must exercise the utmost discretion in her light amours. Was Mr. Morley's suggestion so very different? To be sure, the less said about the lady's birth the better. But to set against that she could bring him not only a handsome dowry but Wellasford itself.

A note from his prospective host suggesting that he bring any of his horses that he wished, especially his hunters, did much to raise his spirits. If hunting was in prospect he was evidently not expected to spend the whole of every day in gentle dalliance. It seemed only sensible to give the thing a decent trial. He fortified himself with the wisdom of several old saws of the 'Nothing venture' school, and completed his preparations for a sojourn in the country.

This time he drove himself in his curricle. No doubt he would be expected to squire the lady in gentle expeditions about the countryside and the curricle would add a touch of

46

panâche to the proceedings. In fact the greys that had been selected for the journey were so fresh that for the first hour they gave him small chance to reflect upon his approaching ordeal. By the time that he was able to spare it a thought the exhilaration of driving at a spanking pace along a good road on a crisp autumn morning had done much to banish his gloomy forebodings.

At least he had not taken Miss Morley in dislike. If she was not precisely the sort of female he admired, at least she was not an antidote. It would be interesting to see how she appeared in modern dress—for presumably she did not spend all her time attired as though she was Mrs. Siddons about to take the stage as Lady Macbeth. And she had seemed to possess an equable disposition and a good deal of dignity, qualities highly desirable in a wife. The prospect, on the whole, might have been very much worse.

For two or three days his visit was quite undistinguishable from the normal country house pattern. He rode or went shooting with his host, drove out when the day was mild with his hostess, spent several hours strolling about the gardens and shrubberies with her, and passed the evenings in playing various card games or just in talking. It was all very comfortable. And at the end of a sennight he found himself obliged to ask Mr. Morley if he had fulfilled his promise of making the situation perfectly clear to his daughter. For there was not the least trace of consciousness in her manner. She treated him in precisely the same friendly fashion that she had used on that first evening, and betrayed none of the apprehension, the female flutterings that he had expected in a young woman who knew herself to be sought in marriage.

Mr. Morley assured him that his daughter was perfectly well acquainted with the purpose of his visit, and was doubtless, in her own fashion, deciding whether or no they would suit. "She is never one for making grand fusses," he explained. And then, suddenly, grinned. "If you *do* decide to make a match of it," he said, "I can promise you a wife who will never enact you a Cheltenham tragedy because you've forgotten some pettifogging engagement. And I'm not sure that *that* isn't better than a great many fashionable accomplishments in which I fear my poor Anna is sadly lacking. Never could see the use of 'em myself, so I didn't insist that she apply herself. I *did* send her to dancing classes, but she hated 'em. She was a stranger—

knew no one—the other girls teased her about her name. Anna stays 'ere—that sort of thing. Which she wasn't used to, being an only one. The only accomplishment for which she showed any aptitude was music. I had her taught to play the harp," he added rather defensively, looking sideways at Julian.

So far had their understanding developed that Julian allowed a crack of laughter to escape him. "Of course you did," he agreed delightedly. "What else could so perfectly complete the picture? Does she play it well?"

Mr. Morley twinkled back at him. "Reasonably well," he decided. "It's a pleasant kind of noise. She sings, too. A small voice, but sweet and true. Could never be persuaded to perform in public, and indeed I doubt if her voice would be sufficiently powerful in a crowded room. You must judge for yourself some evening when she is in the mood."

Miss Morley's appearance in modern dress was neat but not impressive. And as Julian had surmised, she was definitely plump. He wondered if she would grow stout with increasing maturity but recalled hopefully that Mr. Morley's spare frame showed no tendency to corpulence. It was a new idea, though, that behind the serene friendly mask the lady should be assessing *his* merits as a possible husband. He was not at all sure that he cared for it. He had never before given the matter any serious thought but he would have said that all females were on the catch for a husband. After all—what else was there for them to do? And this particular female could scarcely hope to do better. It was not as though he was a fortune hunter, interested only in her expectations. And though he had never been much in the petticoat line he could claim, with all due modesty, that he had never been given cause to doubt his ability to attract such ladies—or lightskirts—as took his fancy. Surely a girl of doubtful pedigree did not aim higher than a Baron? Nevertheless the realisation that she might be weighing his every word and action made him self-conscious and awkward. The only time that he really felt at ease was over dinner. Then, with Miss Morley attired in one of her old-world dresses and her father's presence to remove the tension of tête-à-tête intimacy, he was able to relax into his natural behaviour and enjoy a taste of family life such as he had not known in years.

It seemed to be accepted that for the purpose of 'dressing up for dinner' he was no longer regarded as a stranger. Miss Morley appeared in a succession of different costumes.

A Marriage Arranged

They ranged from the simplicity of early Anglo-Norman to the exotic splendours of the late Plantagenets, and oddly enough she seemed equally at home in all of them. Probably long usage, he supposed, and came to look forward with amused interest to each evening's presentation and to discussing it quite impersonally with father and daughter, realising to some degree how the course of history had dictated the quirks of fashion. During that hour they met as friends, without any tantalising problems of marriage and inheritance to constrain their easy intercourse. And on this particular evening Miss Morley made it plain that her father had reported Julian's puzzlement, for after dinner had run its leisurely course she enquired demurely if the gentlemen would care for a little music and, receiving a polite response, asked one of the footmen to bring in her harp.

She was magnificently attired that night in a fashion that had been popular in the early years of the century. Mr. Morley called it a contouche. There was a loose overdress, made from thick, supple golden taffeta, worn over a soft white under-dress. It was cut low across the bosom and the sleeves ended at the elbow, being turned back to reveal delicate ruffles of the white material. If ever a gown was designed to show off the graceful movements of a woman's hands and arms as she played a harp, that one was. Julian thought there was a glint of deliberate mischief in the lady's eye as she touched the strings, apologised for the delay while she re-tuned the instrument, and enquired their mood.

She played them a Scarlatti sonata, one or two wistful Irish airs and the old English tune, Greensleeves, singing the latter to her own accompaniment in a sweet, almost sleepy little voice. She might have been playing for her own amusement, so little heed did she pay to her audience. Secretly Julian confessed himself surprised, a little entranced. She played and sang a good deal better than he had expected from Mr. Morley's modest account, and he noticed with interest that her hands and arms were beautifully moulded. But it was not just the quality of the performance. It was the atmosphere that she created, in her old-fashioned gown with that soft, creamy skin that made a man wish to smooth his lips over it and her hair simply dressed so that one heavy ringlet came forward over her shoulder and half a dozen loose curls softened the broad brow. For once there was something of enchantment about her, and her very abstraction enhanced that spell. She would not play again, but bade them good night much earlier than was her custom and retired to her own apartments. Mr. Morley and his guest beguiled the evening with a few rubbers of piquet, but Julian found it difficult to focus his attention on the cards.

Had Miss Morley retired early in order to reflect on her situation? Would she reach a decision tonight? And was he himself desirous of going ahead with the scheme? Mr. Morley had suggested a month. Already a week had gone by. Very pleasantly, to be sure, but he felt that it was time that the business which had brought him into Hertfordshire was delicately broached.

Such preoccupations were not conducive to careful judgement in discards, nor to precise calculations of the odds. Mr. Morley beat him handsomely.

Four

Miss Morley herself brought matters to a head the very next day. It was a morning of blustery wind and driving rain. Mr. Morley apologised for deserting his guest on so dismal a day but his duties as a Justice of the Peace obliged him to travel into Ware. Perhaps his lordship would like to play billiards with Anna, who really played reasonably well for a female. Julian glanced across at the lady in smiling enquiry. She said tranquilly that she must first discharge her domestic duties. Perhaps his lordship could amuse himself with a book until this was done. She would look for him in the library as soon as she was free.

She came into the library perhaps an hour later to find him gazing out of the window at the wind-swept trees in the park, and said directly, "I am very willing to play billiards if that is your wish. But if you do not object to it I would rather take this opportunity of talking with you about certain personal matters without fear of interruption."

His lordship, a little staggered by this frank approach, bowed polite assent and drew forward a chair for the lady. She seated herself; very erect, her hands folded quietly in her lap, a sedate figure that yet was imbued with a steady determination that commanded respect, and looked at him thoughtfully for a moment or two as though she was wondering how best to phrase what was in her mind.

"My father told me of your concern that I should be fully informed as to the reason for your visit. I can assure you that he spoke to me quite frankly of the suggestion which he had put to you. But there are one or two circumstances of which *he* is in ignorance, and I feel that it is only fair that you, too, should be fully appraised of all the circumstances before you come to any decision."

If Julian had been a little startled, even mildly shocked by her frank attitude to so delicate a business, he felt nothing but respect for a sense of fair play that was positively masculine. He awaited her further disclosures with considerable interest.

She went on steadily, "I had not thought to marry. In my girlhood, of course, I indulged in the usual romantical dreams of a brave, handsome wooer. But during my London season it was made abundantly clear to me that there was a deal of difference between dreams and real life. To put it bluntly, I did not *take,* and it would be hard to decide whether Aunt Sarah or I was the more thankful when the miserable business came to an end.

"At the same time I am not averse to the married state, and since the possibility was mentioned to me I have given a good deal of thought to it. It seems to me that it might well provide the only means of escape from what is in fact a luxurious prison.

"It is at this point that I must ask you to bear with me patiently. I have seen your growing liking for Papa, and I would not have you think that I do not love him dearly, for indeed I do. Added to which is the immense burden of my gratitude. If he had not chosen to acknowledge me I must have been sent to an orphanage, for my Aunt, kindhearted as she is, would never have dared so far to flout convention. He has been the most generous of fathers and I could not endure to do anything that would hurt him. But his ideas on bringing up a daughter are unusual and absolutely uncompromising. You may have wondered, for instance, why I did not ride with you. It is because Papa will only permit me to ride astride, declaring that side-saddles are unfair to the horse and dangerous for the rider. And you cannot have failed to notice the amount of milk that I am obliged to drink. It is only because of your presence that my meals are not portioned out for me. It is only his tender care for me, you must understand. Concerned because my mother died of the wasting sickness he studied the subject of diet with the same thoroughness that he brings to his business enterprises, and I have been brought up from infancy in conformity with his ideas. You surely did not think that I *like* being as fat as a prize gilt?"

The very crudity of the comparison on the lips of a girl who was usually moderate in speech brought home to Julian the bitterness that lay behind the serene façade. He remembered his sympathy over the milk drinking at their first meeting, and understood something of the frustration of a young, vigorous creature prisoned, however luxuriously, by fetters forged from affection and gratitude. He said, "And the evening dress parade?"

Her rather sombre expression lightened. "Now *that* I have actually come to enjoy. I daresay you are aware that most females like dressing up. And while I do not wholly enter into Papa's infatuation with the things of yester year, I *am* very fond of history and interested in the people who made it. My life here has been very restricted. I enjoy my play-acting—entirely in my own mind, you understand—imagining myself as one or other of the characters whose dresses I wear."

He nodded, thoughtfully. "But since the possibility of marriage arose, you have realised that it might introduce you into a *real* world that is full of interest and opportunity."

"Precisely so, milord." For the first time she seemed to falter a little. Then put up her chin and said, with a hint of defiance, "But only upon certain conditions."

Julian was aware of annoyance. Nothing in the lady's remarks had indicated any appreciation of the honour that he did her in offering marriage to a female of dubious parentage. He had accepted without resentment the implication that he in no way measured up to the paragon of her girlish dreams. But that she should set conditions upon her capitulation was a little too much. He said silkily, "And they are?"

Miss Morley was not insensitive. She said quietly, "I have been clumsy and have made you cross. But if there is to be any thought of marriage between us, surely it must be founded on honesty? Perhaps I should not have spoken of 'conditions'. The word seems to carry an unpleasant taint of blackmail. Let us rather say that if you still deign to honour me with an offer of marriage, I shall beg your understanding and your forbearance."

"And the 'conditions' will still be the same," returned his lordship drily.

There was a soft chuckle for that. "There is small point in dissembling," admitted the lady, "but if you will hear me out I doubt if you will think them too onerous."

He bowed rather stiffly and invited her to proceed.

She said bluntly, "As I apprehend the matter, your main reason for even considering Papa's suggestion was the fact that by marrying me you would eventually regain possession of your family estates. It therefore seems reasonable to suppose that you will be wanting an heir to succeed to those same estates. I see no objection to this and am perfectly willing to play my part in achieving it. In fact, having been an only child myself, I have always thought it would be very pleasant to have quite a large family. But first I would like a few months—a year, perhaps—of freedom."

She seemed to hesitate for a moment, and it was with some constraint that she went on, "I daresay that seems to you an odd kind of notion. You already know that I spent a season in Town with Aunt Sarah when I was eighteen. It was perfectly dreadful. I was gauche and clumsy—and even fatter than I am now. Only just out of the schoolroom where Papa had directed my studies, I had no more sense than to enthuse about the sort of things that interested *him,* which must have made me a shocking bore to most of the gentlemen that I met. Not that I cared a pin for any of them but it is dreadfully lowering to realise that one is a complete failure when all the other girls seem to be pretty and amusing and able to attach any number of beaux without the least effort. Moreover, though this I could not explain to Papa, Aunt Sarah moved only on the fringes of society. She could take me to the Opera and point out the various notables but she did not mix with them, while as for obtaining vouchers for

Almack's I might as well have expected her to frank me through the pearly gates. I have never forgotten it, nor the bitter tears I shed as Aunt Sarah's disappointment became more and more obvious. You may laugh at me if you choose, but ever since then I have cherished a burning ambition to go back and—and *show* them," she finished, on a note of childish fury.

Julian, who had listened to this woeful recital with mild sympathy, said pleasantly, "I shall certainly not laugh at you. In fact I salute your courage in wishing to return to the scene of so much humiliation in order to resume battle. But I cannot see why your very understandable ambition should affect your views on marriage."

"I don't really wish to be married at all," she explained. And then added hastily, "Though I am sure you would be a very creditable sort of husband. The thing is that I don't want to be bothered with *any* sort of husband and certainly not with a baby until I have—have—oh! spread my wings, I suppose. But I can see that it is the only way in which I can hope to escape from Papa's loving tyranny without hurting him."

Julian digested this portion of humble pie with the best grace he could muster. At least, he thought, with a flash of humour, marriage to this young woman would not be quite the dull, bread and butter affair that he had imagined.

"You had better explain to me more precisely what you mean by 'freedom'," he said. The remark was not without malice. She had certainly not spared *his* feelings. He would see how she dealt with *that* home thrust.

She dealt very capably. No doubt she had thought it out beforehand he decided, between resentment and admiration. She said, "I mean that for a few months we should share a roof but not a bed." There she paused for a moment, and when she went on her manner was far less assured. "In such circumstances I suppose I ought to add that I would not take exception to your—your—er—amusements. I would certainly have no right to do so. Only I cannot help hoping that they would not be so blatant as to make me a laughing stock."

She was so serious about it that he was hard put to it not to laugh. It was an intriguing mixture of good sense, naïvety and fair dealing that he was proposing to take to wife! He said solemnly, "I will endeavour to keep my baser instincts within bounds."

Her expression brightened. "Then there is just one more thing," she told him.

He groaned aloud, but the suppressed laughter in his face apparently reassured her. She said slowly, "I know that you love Wellasford dearly. And nothing would please my father better than to have us make our home here with him. But when—if—we marry, you will take me away, won't you? At least for a time. You must see that it would be impossible to maintain the pretence of being properly married under his watchful eye. Besides, I know exactly what I want to do as soon as I am free, and *that* would be even more impossible."

"And what *do* you intend to do?" he enquired quizzically.

She twinkled back at him but shook her head. "*That* I shall not tell you, milord. I do not *think* that you will disapprove, but you might unwittingly betray me to my father. And after all, I have not yet promised to obey."

He looked dubious. "I could not support you in anything that would earn your father's serious disapproval," he said soberly.

She was swift to understand. "Of course you could not. Just trivial things like not drinking milk and eating up my pudding," she placated.

Julian felt a twinge of pity. Poor child!

Such petty regulations should have been left behind in nursery days. "Very well," he conceded. "And if you mean to make a stir in fashionable circles you will want to do a deal of shopping. We had best hire a house in Town for the time being. Later on, perhaps, we might buy one."

"An excellent idea. Though if you have no objection I would prefer to spend the first few weeks with my old governess. She is now retired, but she was always used to enter into my feelings about the amount of food that I was obliged to eat. You will readily appreciate that I would prefer to make my second début in a slightly less imposing shape."

"Provided you take no foolish risks with your health—yes."

She chuckled. "That I can safely promise. I have a very healthy appetite. You will not find me subscribing to such ridiculous reducing diets as those that recommend drinking vinegar and eating only dry biscuits. But I do believe that strict moderation—and little of the detested milk—will have a beneficial effect."

He was rather doubtful about the practicability of this part of her scheme, pointing out that her father was often in Town on business and would think it very odd if she was away from home every time that he called, but she shrugged off this very reasonable objection. Surely he was capable of inventing a credible excuse if it became necessary? But it wouldn't. Papa could be trusted not to intrude upon people so newly wed unless actually invited to do so. When he still demurred at what seemed to him as unnecessary complication in a business that was already awkward enough, she said simply, "I shall be beginning a new life. I do not want anyone to see me as I am now. Not the servants in the fine house that you are going to hire, not your friends, not even you."

He laughed till he choked and had to be patted on the back before he could explain that it was his own lowly place in this hierarchy that was so funny, and that he would not permit her to lower his crest still further by explaining what she had really meant. "For you have a wonderful knack of administering a handsome setdown in the guise of kindly explanation," he told her.

Somehow, although the question had neither been asked nor answered, it seemed to be mutually understood that the marriage was acceptable to both the contracting parties.

Five

Except for the need to find a suitable Town
house there was no particular reason for delay.
In fact the three people most concerned were
agreed that the sooner the business was settled, the better. It would be a quiet ceremony,
both bride and groom being singularly devoid
of close relations. Julian rather thought he
had some distant cousins in the north of
England. At least he could remember Mama
saying that they lived in Alnwick because his
fancy had been caught by her descriptions of
the ancient castle. But since that was twenty
years ago and he had never actually met the
cousins he did not feel it incumbent upon him

to invite them to his wedding. The bride's uncle and aunt must naturally be invited and their fourteen-year-old daughter would be overjoyed to act as bride's maiden, but Julian found himself in something of a difficulty over finding a groomsman. Newly returned to England he had not yet had time to pick up the threads of old friendships.

This was a problem that was still unsolved when he set out for London on his house hunting expedition, armed with a good deal of advice from his prospective father-in-law as to the choice of a suitable locality. Julian had pokered up a trifle when Mr. Morley had started to express his views on this head, but he soon discovered that the speaker did not care a pin for fashion and was concerned only with the health-giving aspects of certain neighbourhoods as opposed to the insidious dangers of others. He listened patiently to a long dissertation of the fever-breeding miasmas that were inevitably associated with low-lying land, and was aware of a growing sympathy with his bride's rebellion against her father's preoccupation with matters of health and nutrition, however sensible and well-intentioned his advice.

He reached London just as dusk was falling and repaired to Fenton's Hotel, where he dined early and settled down in the coffee room with a pile of newspapers to study the descriptions of the several commodious and elegantly furnished houses whose owners were prepared to hire them to carefully selected tenants at exorbitant prices. None of them was precisely what he wanted, and he had a strong suspicion that in some cases the descriptions were deliberately misleading. He was just deciding that it might be best to employ an agent in the task when he heard his name spoken and looked up to see a sturdy, pleasant-faced young man regarding him with the half doubtful smile of one who is not wholly sure of his recognition.

"You don't remember me. John Merridew. But surely I am not mistaken. It *is* Julian Wellasford?"

Julian sprang up with an exclamation of pleasure. "It is indeed. Why, Johnnie! Small wonder that I did not recognise you. You were no more than a scrubby schoolboy when last we met. What is it? Ten years? Twelve? But come. We must crack a bottle on this, and you must tell me all the family news. I most sincerely trust that you have no pressing engagement for tonight."

Mr. Merridew had no engagement. His diffidence vanishing in face of Julian's patent delight in the chance meeting, he confided that he had only come up to Town to give Caro a hand. "You'll remember m'sister, Caroline? 'Bout your age, ain't she? Married out of the schoolroom as they say, and her husband died a year ago, soon after Papa. Just has the one boy. Thing is she's decided to let her Town house and move into a smaller place. Says she wants to hold household for the boy's sake, though I must say I can't see why—But so it is," he broke off awkwardly.

As a matter of fact he understood his sister's motives pretty well. If she stayed in the Portman Square house she could scarcely shuffle off all the responsibility for twin sisters and for the small brother whose belated arrival into the Merridew family had robbed them of their mother. Roy could be sent to school, but Phyllida and Chloe, approaching seventeen and quite deliciously pretty would be very much in the way. When they had paid her a brief visit during the summer, Caro had realised at once that their youth and freshness made her own frail, wistful beauty appear strained and faded. Stupid people might even enquire if they were her daughters—and at thirty-two it was just barely possible, though naturally she never admitted to her actual age. Yet she could not openly deny them the shelter of her roof. It would sort ill with a carefully cultivated reputation for sweetness and self-sacrifice. Much better to let the Portman Square house, though she would sadly miss its spacious comfort. The tiny house in North Audley Street could only just accommodate a pathetically brave widow who was striving to do her best for her child. People would simply suppose that Sir Marmaduke's debts had been heavier than expected, and no one would ask her to house two growing girls and a younger brother in that doll's house.

Yes. An astute creature, his sister Caro, decided Johnnie tolerantly. No harm done, really. The twins and Roy could very well spend another year in Devonshire with Aunt Maria, who adored them all. The girls would be disappointed but they were really far too young to be introduced into the sophisticated circles that Caro favoured. He could not help admiring his sister's tactics, however selfish, and the effortless ease with which she manipulated circumstances so that she actually appeared to be their victim. But naturally family loyalty forbade him to share these opinions with Julian. He said only that his sister had decided that a smaller house would be perfectly adequate to her simple needs—

never dreaming how carefully that choice
phrase had been instilled into his memory by
that sister's careful and painstaking repeti-
tion—and what with Portman Square all
swept and garnished for inspection by would-
be tenants, North Audley Street too small for
comfort, and his sister, in any case, gone to a
theatre party with friends, he had decided to
seek refuge at Fenton's.

They then indulged in the nostalgic pleasures of 'Do you remember?' interspersed with
brief reports on the present employment and
marital status of the Merridew family and
such of the Rectory children as came within
Johnnie's orbit. It was a delicate business
because Julian knew that the Merridews had
been as poverty-pinched as the Wellasfords.
Johnnie's parents had been a pair of charming scatterbrains, and the production of eight
children, all of whom had survived infancy,
must have put a severe strain on the family
resources. However, it emerged that all five
of the older children were comfortably established. Johnnie himself had a good post as
baliff for a wealthy city merchant who had
retired from business and purchased a vast
but sadly run-down country estate.

"A decent sort of fellow," was Johnnie's
view. "As ignorant of good farming practice

as a day-old pup, but has the sense to know it.
What he wanted was a man he could rely on
to do the job for him. No expense spared
where the land is concerned, pays me a generous salary and is very reasonable over my
taking time off on such occasions as the present. Suits me nicely. I was never bookish so
there was no hope of my going into the Church,
like Paul, or the Law, like Sammy." He
grinned suddenly. "What old Satterthwaite—
my employer—really wanted was a chap who
was just stupid enough to be honest. We get
on splendidly."

Johnnie might not be bookish but he seemed
to be a shrewd judge of men, thought Julian
appreciatively. And presently it transpired
that he owed his present position to the good
offices of Mr. Morley.

"He bought Combe House, y'know, after
Mama died, and paid a very fair price for it.
My father had lost all interest—completely
broken up. Only too anxious to get away from
the place. He took the twins and Roy and
went off to Devonshire to Aunt Maria. Well—
what else *could* he do, and Roy just a babe,
and puny at that? But it put the rest of us in a
bit of a fix. Sammy and me, any way. And it
was Mr. Morley that helped us both out.
Which he had no call to do. I daresay you're

at outs with him, snapping up Wellasford when your Papa played wily beguiled—but no matter. You'll have to forgive me—I never could run mute. What I'm trying to say is that Nathaniel Morley's a good sort. I owe him a lot—and I'll not forget it."

He fell silent for a moment, contemplating the virtues of the absent Mr. Morley, then remembered that Julian had small cause to love the gentleman who had taken over his beloved Wellasford and went on to speak of other members of his family. Mr. Morley was discreetly banished.

Julian was quite surprised at his own sense of satisfaction, evoked by Johnnie's praise of his future father-in-law. It was pleasant to have his own growing liking for the older man so amply supported by someone who knew nothing of the terms on which they stood, but for some odd reason it made it rather awkward to speak openly of his present plans. When Johnnie, having exhausted his own news budget, enquired what Julian was doing now and how long he was fixed in Town, he hedged slightly, saying that his present object was to find a place to live.

Johnnie promptly embarked on a list of bachelor apartments, snug little pieds-à-terre, possibly the Albany, if the dibs were in tune, though *there* one might have to wait for a vacancy.

Julian was obliged to break across this helpful discourse, explaining that he had something rather more commodious in mind, which caused his friend to regard him with a suddenly speculative eye.

"H'm. Something larger. How much larger? What I mean is, know you're not married nor even promised. Can't think *how* I know, but I do. Daresay someone was talking about you being back in England." A sudden notion struck him. He said cheerfully, "If you're thinking of setting up some charming little barque of frailty in a discreet establishment, then Hans Town is your place, or perhaps Bloomsbury or Pimlico. Was you thinking of buying or renting? If you buy I'd advise you to keep your own hands on the deeds. Some of these little ladies, you know, have surprisingly acquisitive instincts."

Julian could not help grinning. Johnnie's knowledge of the amenities offered by the various quarters of London seemed to match Mr. Morley's, though undoubtedly he viewed them from a different angle.

"So I have been credibly informed," he returned, and drew a reproving mouth. "But you have it wrong. What I am looking for is a respectable family house in a healthy district. And I wish to rent rather than buy. Furnished if possible. We want to take time to look about us before we decide where we would like to settle, and a hired furnished house seems to be the answer. One very soon wearies of hotels—even good ones."

Johnnie did not even hear this final platitude. His eyes had rounded to that revealing 'we' and he had heard the rest of the explanation in very random fashion. He said breathlessly, "Never tell me you're thinking of getting leg-shackled? Well, by George!" in answer to Julian's smiling sketch of a bow. "This is beyond anything great. How is it that the news is not generally known?"

"It has not been formally announced as yet, and is to be a very quiet affair. You will understand that at this stage I prefer to say no more. But if you can help me find the house I am looking for, you will put me very much in your debt. There is nothing in the advertisements at all suited to my requirements."

Johnnie embarked on this new quest with touching enthusiasm. It seemed positively unkind to tease him with Mr. Morley's endless specifications, but Julian found the temptation irresistible. Johnnie accepted them all, as a good hound accepts a check and a fresh cast. Suitable neighbourhoods were suggested in swift succession. It was not until Julian threw in a final teaser, "A fairly modern house, of course. None of your old London residences, riddled with rat-holes and over-run by cock-coaches. Everything clean and fresh and up-to-date," that he suddenly stopped dead, threw Julian a very wary glance, and then said slowly, "It seems to me, old fellow, that you could do worse than cast an eye over m'sister Caro's place in Portman Square. Mind, it may be bigger than you want, and I daresay she's asking a high figure for it, though that's none of my business. But at least I can vouch for its comfort and cleanliness and it's no more than ten years old."

After further discussion the idea emerged as a sound one. Johnnie supplied some rather vague information as to the number of reception rooms and bedrooms that the house contained, though he was naturally ignorant as to domestic offices and servants' quarters. He regretted that he could not spare the time to take the prospective tenant on a personally conducted tour of inspection but furnished his sister's address in North Audley Street and added that if Julian didn't mind getting up betimes next day he would go along with him and introduce him to Caro's solicitor before setting out on his journey. "Don't care to put upon old Satterthwaite's good nature," he explained apologetically, "or I'd take you along to Caro's myself and I daresay she'd have it all fixed up in a trice. But she don't get up much before noon and I want to be well on my way by then."

Julian said that the house sounded very promising, and added that, while he looked forward to renewing his acquaintance with Lady Holroyd at some future date, he would prefer to settle business matters with her lawyers.

Johnnie agreeing that there was a good deal of sense in this view, they drank another bottle to their fortunate reunion and presently parted in great amity.

A thorough inspection of the house in Portman Square proved mainly satisfactory. Julian did not greatly care for the decorative schemes or for the ornate furnishings, but he supposed that when one hired a furnished house one must expect that sort of thing. The young clerk to whom had been assigned the duty of showing him over the premises was much shocked by this ill-informed attitude. "Perhaps, milord, you are more accustomed to living in the country," he suggested in superior tones, "where the furnishings are old-fashioned and solid, built to last. But Milady Holroyd would have none of that. Everything always of the first stare for her ladyship. The rooms are re-decorated every year, the old furniture turned out and the salons re-furnished in the very latest mode."

Small wonder, then, that she found herself obliged to economise, thought Julian, and a pity that she had not devoted some of her attention to the servants' quarters. He knew that his concern with such an unimportant matter was quite out of step with accepted practice. Probably it stemmed from his army experience. He had come to believe that if a man was good enough to serve alongside you, to share your dangers and discomforts, then he deserved to enjoy all the amenities that you could provide. And surely the same code should apply in domestic life? The cramped, stuffy and dingy accommodation in the attics and basement of Lady Holroyd's sumptuous home would not do for *his* servants. But that, he remembered comfortably, could safely be left to the management of the lady of the house. It never even occurred to him that she might not share his views.

In this opinion he was perfectly right. An expedition to Town in the company of Mr.

and Miss Morley revealed that both agreed with him, not only about the staff quarters but also about the furnishings, which Mr. Morley unhesitatingly stigmatised as, "Trash!" He added that he would rather risk his neck over a regular stitcher than entrust himself to the fragile gilt chairs.

Miss Morley said placidly, "I daresay they are all the crack but I confess I don't care for them. Chairs should be comfortable, and never mind smartness."

Her Papa grunted that 'crack' was about the best word to describe them, since you could never seat any but the most sylph-like of guests on such abominations without expecting them to do just that.

Julian grinned appreciatively but his daughter paid no heed. She said thoughtfully, "Well it is fortunate that the house is too big for us. We can store all the things we dislike in the attics and use the nursery and school-room floor for our servants. That will leave ample accommodation for the two of us—and for one or two especially favoured guests," she added, bestowing upon her Papa a smile of such warmth and sweetness that his voice was quite gruff as he told her that she need not think that he meant to thrust himself upon them every time he came to Town.

"Well, not just at first," she agreed. "I daresay we shall take a little time to get used to being married. But at least you must promise to be our very first house guest."

Which left her father highly gratified and her betrothed husband filled with amazement at the ways and wiles of women. Who could have imagined that the girl who had spoken to him so frankly in the library at Wellasford was capable of such subtle manoeuvring?

Six

The marriage was arranged for early January, the bride having expressed a wish to spend Yule-tide in her father's home. All three were content to pass the festive season quietly, the preceding weeks having been busy ones for all of them. Julian had been obliged to go off into Surrey to take order over the Pittsfield estate and had delegated to Mr. Morley the responsibility of advising his daughter over the re-furbishing of the Portman Square house. Some lively arguments ensued, Mr. Morley's tastes naturally leading him to favour the antique, which Anna declared was quite out of place in a modern

house. She was able to restrain him from
embarking upon a number of structural alterations, pointing out that the terms of the
lease forbade them, and they eventually
reached a happy compromise as to the deco-
ration and furnishing of the principal rooms.
The walls were to be hung with damask in
pleasing shades of cream, palest gold and
green, colours which would set off the choice
pieces of Chippendale and the chairs that
Papa had just discovered by a new fellow
named Hepplewhite who had a small business in Cripplegate. The gimcrack objects
that had earned his dislike were carefully
stored away in the attics together with several mirrors and pictures in ornate gilded
frames. Painters were set to work to freshen
up the basement and the schoolroom floor,
and as soon as this was done a housekeeper
and a butler were engaged. Having given due
consideration to the accommodation provided
for them and to the generous scale of the
wages suggested, these formidable personages
were very willing to recommend certain
trusted underlings to serve a gentleman who
obviously demanded the best and was prepared to pay for it. Having set in hand one or
two improvements in the stables and coachman's quarters and announced firmly that

the Wellasford second coachman would take charge of that department, father and daughter were able to leave Town in the comfortable knowledge that all was in train for the smooth running of the household. Julian, returning from Surrey, spent a couple of nights in Town, was duly impressed by the miracles that had been wrought in his absence, and arrived in Hertfordshire eager to express his appreciation and gratitude for Mr. Morley's good offices.

The three of them spent a pleasant evening, well content to be together again, Julian vowing that after what they had achieved in Portman Square he would certainly strive to engage Mr. Morley's interest in schemes for his Surrey house and confessing that it was a little too Spartan even for his simple tastes. "Though there are one or two pieces there that may interest *you*, sir. Been there since the place was built, in Elizabeth's day."

He did his best to satisfy the connoisseur's eager interest, but ended in a laughing admission of ignorance and a suggestion that Mr. Morley had best come and see for himself.

"And that is looking a long way ahead," sighed Mr. Morley, "what with Christmas almost upon us and your wedding to follow so soon after. Which reminds me that we must draft a notice for the papers. We might do that tonight, after Anna's gone to bed."

Whereupon Anna, remarking with perfect good humour that she could take a hint as well as any one, bade them a placid good night.

Mr. Morley hitched his chair a little closer to Julian's and dropped his voice to a confidential note. "Fact is, there's one thing I'd like to tell you," he said slowly. "Never meant to. The people concerned are dead and gone and I thought to let the story die with them. But somehow, seeing you and Anna so easy together and her so busy and interested over the house, let alone your asking me down to your Surrey place, I'm beginning to feel mean. Maybe if I can explain things to you I'll feel better."

"Certainly, sir, if that is your wish," returned Julian. "Though as for feeling mean I can imagine no man with less cause."

Mr. Morley grunted. "Wait till you hear. It concerns Wellasford." And as Julian's brows flicked upwards in surprise, "You must surely sometimes have wondered why I insisted that no other place would do."

"Now that you remark upon it, I did indeed wonder at the time. But it is so long ago—and so much has happened since—that I had forgot. Except to wonder once or twice because it was out of character. You are a shrewd business man. Wellasford has cost you dear and gives little return. Yes. I realise it now. I *have* wondered."

"It was for Anastasia," said Mr. Morley simply, and his use of the girl's full name indicated the solemnity of his mood. "I wanted it for her. I told you once that her father's blood was as good as yours. It was, in fact, linked with yours. He was that Humphrey Wellasford who fell at Wandewash. Your father's second cousin. One should not speak ill of the dead, and in his way he was a nice enough lad. Handsome, high-spirited and charming—but utterly spoilt and wholly irresponsible. Even in those days I could have bought him up twice over, but socially our family was quite beneath his touch. Merchant stock—trade." There was a note of bitterness in his voice for old remembered wrongs as he added, "Always willing to borrow from us, the nobility—aye, and even royalty, as far back as history records. And genial as anyone could wish until their immediate necessities were relieved. Well—we have our pride, too. I did my possible to keep my sister from young Wellasford, knowing that nothing honourable could come of his attentions. But I was a busy man. And I never dreamed that, strictly reared as she had been, she would consent to clandestine meetings and permit herself to be seduced with an easy promise of marriage when he should return to England. I should have cared for her better, as I *have* cared for her daughter. And when I stood by her grave and knew her child was doubly orphaned I resolved that some day, if it lay within my power, that child should inherit all that was her due by right of blood. That was why only Wellasford would do."

For a moment he seemed to be brooding over his determination and its outcome. Then, with an attempt at lightness, he went on, "It was Anna's fancy to have her baby named Anastasia. Outlandish to my way of thinking. But it emerged that Humphrey's second name, the one that his friends used, was Stacy. Anastasia was the nearest she could come to naming her child for both of them."

Julian said slowly, "If I had been in your position—had your abilities—your determination—I hope I would have decided as you did. You have done nobly by your sister's child and can have no qualms of conscience over an undertaking so amply fulfilled. In fact," he smiled across at Mr. Morley, "as things have fallen out, you have achieved even more than you planned, for Anastasia will now have both the name to which she is entitled by birth and the rank which she could not have inherited. Does she know the truth of her parentage?"

"Only that she is illegitimate. Not the identity of her father. Tell her if you wish—I shall not. As for the future, the degree of relationship is remote. No need to fear that the pair of you will breed moonlings."

A true word, thought Julian, wryly amused. Or anything else either, under the present dispensation. He preserved a sympathetic countenance and devoted himself to distracting his host from the sorrowful memories that their talk had evoked.

He found the Christmas arrangements at this new style Wellasford of absorbing interest. He had vivid memories of the tenants' parties of his childhood. These had always been held on St. Stephen's day, and a number of items that had graced the festive board on the preceding day made a second appearance in support of the mounds of brawn and spiced beef and the jellies and syllabubs designed to tempt the ladies. The proceedings opened with a tea for the children, a very decorous affair, with hovering parents anxious to ensure that

their offspring did ample justice to buns and
mince pies, spice bread and plum cake, while
at the same time maintaining the family
honour by the nicety of their table manners
and the general propriety of their behaviour.
The children then found some relief from this
unnatural state of affairs in games of Hood-
man Blind and Snapdragon, after which,
stuffed, exhausted or merely subdued by repeated admonitions, they were relegated to
the benches that had been set up in the Great
Hall while their parents took their turn at
the well furnished tables. The proceedings
ended with dancing, in which all the household and estate servants joined. Julian could
still remember the picture presented by his
tiny Mama dancing with the tall and portly
Graves—the butler—as tradition demanded.
He had always thought it a pity that Papa's
other engagements inevitably called him away
before this stage of the party was reached.
This much older Julian could better appreciate Papa's difficulties. Even a moonless return to Town must have seemed positively
inviting as compared to the hazards of steer-
ing all eighteen stone of Mrs. Morris through
the intricacies of the dance. He realised, too,
that it was thanks to Mama that those
memorable feasts had been so amply provid-

ed, and speculated a little as to how it had been managed. Certainly he expected to see something of the same sort, probably on a more lavish scale.

Anna enlightened him. "Papa would tell you that those are gentry ways," she said, schooling her lips to primness though her eyes quizzed him wickedly, "and he would not so far presume. But it is a shame to tease you," she relented. "The truth is that he does not care for large parties, and despite his love of tradition he is actually inclined to be ill-at-ease when faced with the tenants and their families in force. He discharges his hospitable dues towards them with gifts of meat and tea and money for the children. But he *does* enjoy the visit of the waits on Christmas Eve. Most of them are village folk and have nothing to do with Wellasford, and with them he is quite at ease. You will see."

There had been a hard frost and provision for the refreshment of the expected visitors had been made accordingly. Julian eyed the big table that had been brought in and set up in front of the blazing log fire with interest and approval. There were platters laden with wedges of giblet pie and generous hunks of plum cake. And as the last notes of 'The holly and the ivy' died away and the singers broke into the traditional greeting of 'God bless the master of this house' the maids came hurrying in with trays of hot meat patties and steaming jugs of mulled ale, while Anna presided over a jug of hot chocolate for such members of the party as were judged too young for this potent brew. Small wonder that there was a brightening of eyes in frost-reddened faces and even a discreet smacking of lips as the singers trooped in, their heavy boots clattering on the old stone floor. There were a dozen men and perhaps twice as many youngsters, and having chorused their seasonal greetings they needed no urging to fall to with a will, wandering about the hall in obvious content, at ease and interested as they ate and drank, returning to the table for replenishment of mugs or for more food. Occasionally an inquisitive lad was called to order by his elders for fingering the ancient weapons with which the walls were hung. Once Mr. Morley lifted down a wheel-lock musket and demonstrated how the sparks were produced to ignite the powder in the priming pan and fire the charge. Even the pleasure of eating too much rich food palled in the face of this entertainment, and there was a concerted sigh of regret when he replaced the weapon.

A Marriage Arranged

Julian held himself a little aloof, having no least desire to encroach upon the position of his host. Fortunately there were only two among the visitors who were known to him. He could not help noticing how easily Mr. Morley moved from group to group with a pleasant word for every one seeming to adapt himself without difficulty to the slow-paced rustic talk and the rather laboured jokes. He was obviously well-liked, and not, Julian thought, just for his generosity. One mán asked his advice in connection with a carrier's business that he hoped to start in the spring. Mr. Morley asked one or two shrewd questions and then suggested that Packard should come up and have a further talk with him before he committed himself too far. It seemed to Julian a curious anomaly that a man who could rub shoulders so comfortably with his humbler neighbours should have difficulty in achieving the same relationship with his tenants. It must be abundantly clear that every one was very much better off under Mr. Morley's enlightened suzerainty than ever they had been while his father ruled. But country roots struck deep and were not always controlled by self-interest. Thorpes and Richmonds, Boltons and Goodisons had farmed Wellasford acres time out of mind. There had been good landlords and bad, but yeoman farmer and peasant alike had accepted changing fortune philosophically and had followed the lord of the manor to war whenever occasion demanded. They had served and suffered and some of them had died together in ancient quarrels from Agincourt to Naseby. Perhaps there was still a link, a dumb, scarce comprehended loyalty. If that were so, his forthcoming marriage might well serve to bind together the old regime with the new. He might, in a dozen insignificant ways, help to smooth Mr. Morley's path. He did not even find it strange that the thought should give him considerable pleasure—he who three short months earlier had certainly regarded Mr. Morley as an interloper. He dismissed idle speculation anent the peculiarities of human nature and went to lend a hand in the dispensing of hospitality.

Aunt Sarah Woodstock came to keep New Year with her brother, accompanied by her husband and daughter. Julian had the grace to feel slightly ashamed of himself for finding all three of them sadly boring. Perhaps, having found the society of Miss Morley and her father both pleasant and stimulating, he had expected too much. Mrs. Woodstock, alas, was distinctly commonplace. Kindhearted she

might be but she was totally lacking in force
of character. Deference to the superiority of
the masculine mind was possibly an admirable attitude in a female. Carried to extremes
it could make her appear devoid of even common sense, the more so since her husband
and her brother frequently expressed contra-
dictory opinions and she found herself in the
awkward position of trying to subscribe to
both. Mr. Woodstock—Uncle William—was a
hide-bound Tory. He quoted Dr. Johnson's dic-
tum that 'the first Whig was the Devil', and
was firmly convinced that any measure designed to ease the lot of the labouring classes
was a step on the road to revolution. Conse-
quently he was often at outs with the more
humane Mr. Morley.

Julian's chief discomfort arose from the
exaggerated respect in which Aunt Sarah
held the nobility. She made it plain that she
thought her niece had captured a matrimonial
prize of the first stare, and her conversation
was so liberally punctuated with 'milords'
and 'Lord Wellasfords' that Julian had to
restrain an impulse to bow his acknowledge-
ments every time she addressed him. She
was for ever instructing her daughter as to
the proper way to speak and behave in his
presence, and when he actually heard her

advising Anna to use more deference towards him he was hard put to it to keep his tongue.

So far as an opinion delivered mainly in grunts and snorts could be interpreted, Mr. Woodstock appeared at first to share his wife's view that Anastasia was doing very well for herself, but this comfortable state of affairs was short-lived. On a wet afternoon when escape out of doors was impossible he subjected the bridegroom elect to a searching interrogation as to his past life, his present occupation and future plans that might have been thought presumptuous even in the bride's father. Julian endured it as best he might until Mr. Woodstock, having failed to unearth anything discreditable, summed up pompously, "Can't think why ever you sold out of the army. Best life in the world for a man of spirit. Not even as though you was needed here at home."

That final jibe was the last straw heaped on Julian's mounting indignation. He longed to ask Uncle William if this opinion was based on his personal experience of military life, but to match the fellow in discourtesy could only reflect on himself. He swallowed his wrath, though the cutting drawl that marred his usually pleasant voice would have betrayed him to his intimates. "Do you know," he said silkily, "I think it must have been because I got tired of killing Englishmen."

"Englishmen?" snorted Mr. Woodstock, whose understanding was not of the swiftest.

"Oh—I daresay there may have been a few Scots and Irish among them," elaborated Julian helpfully, "for all they called themselves Americans."

"English! Americans! Why, you impudent young dog, they were rebels. Damned traitors! And deserved a traitor's end. A clean, honourable death in battle was too good for them. Should have been hung, drawn and quartered. And you to complain of killing a few when it was no more than your plain duty. Just the sort of sloppy sentiment that will be the ruin of the army, same as this Frenchman, Rooso or whatever his name is—the one that Nat is for ever on about—will be the ruin of sound government. You should be ashamed of yourself."

Julian was. Though not for the reason that Mr. Woodstock had suggested. He returned a soothing answer but it did not serve to appease Uncle William. Thereafter he was treated with coldness, Mr. Woodstock avoiding him as far as possible and keeping any necessary conversational exchanges brief. Julian was divided between relief and penitence, but on the whole relief won.

Apart from this small breeze the days passed uneventfully. Aunt Sarah fussed over Anna, taking her aside for little confidential talks and trying to persuade her to change her mind over the 'very peculiar' dress that she had decided to wear for her wedding. For Anna, to her Papa's intense gratification, had chosen one of the gowns from his collection. Julian and Mr. Morley spent a morning closeted with Mr. Edgewick over settlements, Uncle William remained frostily aloof and young Corinna hung adoringly around the bridegroom until Anna laughingly declared that if the child were a few years older she would have cause for jealousy.

"But don't grow *too* puffed up in your own conceit," she added mischievously, "for I fear that it is chiefly the glamour of your rank that holds her entranced. Even *I* have risen considerably in her esteem now that I am betrothed to a 'real live lordship'," and slipped away to answer a call from Aunt Sarah before he could favour her with his views on toad-eaters and tuft-hunters.

Seven

Johnnie Merridew obligingly consented to act as groomsman to his old friend, undertaking to escort him to church in good time on the fateful day and to see the knot well and truly tied. He apologised diffidently that he did not care to ask for longer leave of absence since his employer was already over-generous in that respect, and added that he looked forward with much pleasure to making the acquaintance of the bride.

In his new knowledge of the Morley family's standing in the neighbourhood, Julian was not really surprised to find the little church packed to the doors and a group of village folk gathered outside, daring the January chill in order to see the bride arrive. What *did* a little surprise him was Johnnie's startled and patently admiring, "By Jove!" as Anna came up the aisle on her father's arm. There was no time for *him* to take note of her appearance, though he recognised the gravity in the clear grey eyes as he smiled down at her and guessed that she was finding the ceremony more of an ordeal than she had anticipated. Then he himself was caught up in the solemn opening phrases.

There did not seem to be any logical cause for the odd sense of guilt that possessed him as he listened. The agreement which he and Anna had made was only temporary. Sooner or later they meant to fulfill all the purposes for which, said the Church, marriage had been ordained. So why feel uneasy about it? He spent so long pondering this point that a sudden pause in the proceedings caught him unprepared. Johnnie was looking at him anxiously, the priest enquiringly. The echo of words dimly heard roused him to full awareness. Hastily he said, "I will," in a very determined way, and thereafter succeeded in keeping his mind on the business in hand.

It was not until they came out of church that he understood Johnnie's irreverent, "By

Jove!" It was then that the admiration writ plain in the faces of the bystanders as they pressed about bride and groom to offer their congratulations and good wishes, made him take his first real look at his wife.

Man-like, he could not have attempted to describe her gown. He *did* notice that her hair was dressed in a different fashion, because it made her look taller, and that the smooth fair skin was flawless in the searching January sunlight. But it was her serene dignity that caught the imagination. It was difficult to say just how the impression was achieved, but in her silken bridal robes with her head held high she moved like a queen; a queen at ease among her friends, relaxed and beloved.

Settling himself beside her in the waiting carriage, he tried, rather awkwardly, to express his sentiments. "That is a magnificent gown, my dear," he told her, supremely tactless. "I have never seen you look better."

He was somewhat taken aback to hear her gasp of laughter, hastily stifled, but in fact his ineptitude served him well. She said demurely, "It is naturally an object with me to please your lordship's fastidious taste. I am gratified that my *dress* finds favour in your eyes."

His lordship eyed her thoughtfully. "Dear me," he said. "What a shrew I have married. Yes. I see. I should rather have praised your looks first and the gown second. But you must remember that I am not practised in the arts of gallantry. I will study to improve."

That won him an engaging twinkle. "At least you are not dull-witted," she told him kindly. "And after a week of Uncle William—"

It was his turn to laugh. He flung up one hand in mock surrender as he exclaimed, "Cry Pax! You have certainly had the better of that encounter and I will concede victory. Let me see if I can do better. You look quite delightfully. So much so that your appearance startled my groomsman into a most unbecoming expression of admiration. In church, too."

She flushed vividly. "Truly?" she breathed, her face alight with pleasure.

"Yes indeed. And he is quite a connoisseur, you know, because his sisters are extremely pretty."

She said shyly, "You will think me very foolish to refine so much on what was probably only Mr. Merridew's kindness. But you see no one has ever admired my looks or paid me compliments, and I find it quite a delightful sensation."

"Well that is quite your own fault for shutting yourself away from Society," he told her briskly. "And we are going to put an end to all that. As for kindness—no such thing. The fellow positively licked his lips over you. Most improper!"

Perhaps that was a little exaggerated, but Johnnie would not mind. And he must do what he could to brighten the day for his bride. So much at least he owed her.

Fulfilling his duties manfully, Johnnie did his best to enliven the wedding breakfast by entertaining Aunt Sarah and Uncle William, but it was an uphill task. Conversation does not flourish when one participant agrees with everything that is said and another flatly contradicts most of it. Unfortunately, too, Mr. Morley was in subdued mood, the realisation having come to him that, with Anna's going, his life would be vastly changed. It was in an attempt to give his father-in-law's thoughts a more cheerful direction that Julian introduced the topic of the bride's dress. Johnnie seconded him nobly, enquiring with genuine interest about the material from which it was made, saying that he had never seen anything quite like it before.

Mr. Morley revived splendidly under this stimulus. "Nor you wouldn't," he nodded with mild triumph. "Specially woven for me. And I'd not like to count how many pieces were spoiled before I was suited. It's samite."

His audience studied the beautiful fabric in respectful silence, though none of them had heard of it before; a thick silk, its texture slightly roughened by the fine threads of gold that were woven into it. The dress was loosely cut so that it hung in heavy folds from the shoulders, bearing some resemblance to a modern sacque. It was this that had finally reconciled Aunt Sarah to Anna's choice, though she had taken strong exception to the band of glowing embroidery that bordered the rounded neck and matched the colours in the jewelled girdle. Barbaric. Oriental, said her brother. Aunt Sarah shuddered delicately. A bride should wear only white.

"It was copied from a dress thought to have been worn by Berengaria of Navarre," explained Mr. Morley, now happily mounted on his hobby-horse. "Stand up, my dear, and let us see it properly."

Anna obeyed him, turning about with that total absence of self-consciousness that Julian had come to expect of her, so that they could all study the beautiful thing.

"It has always been quite my favourite," she said gently, touching the white silk with loving fingers, "though I have never worn it because it would soil so easily, so I thought I had best make the most of this opportunity."

She narrowed her eyes engagingly at her father, who said cheerfully, "We could always have it copied again. But I *do* regret that you refused to complete the picture by wearing your hair loose."

She chuckled. "Aunt Sarah would have washed her hands of me if I had done anything so outlandish. She found it quite difficult enough to resign herself to my wearing colours. Didn't you, love?"

Uncle William felt that he had been left out of the conversation for long enough. In any case his wife's views were of no interest.

"And who was Berengaria of Navarre?" he demanded belligerently. "What has she to say to anything?"

"She was a Queen of England," said Mr. Morley. "The only one who never set foot in the country."

"Oh! History," exclaimed young Corinna, greatly daring in this adult assembly but eager to draw attention to herself. "Fusty old stuff!"

Maternal devotion impelled Aunt Sarah to intervene before her husband could express his views or the desirability of children being seen and not heard, and preferably only rarely seen.

"Which one was she?" she asked brightly.

Mr. Morley sighed. "She married Coeur-de-Lion," he said patiently. "And he was too busy crusading and subduing rebellious vassals to look after a wife."

"But undoubtedly England's greatest king," concluded Uncle William in a voice that brooked no argument.

Since no one wished to mar the harmony of the wedding feast, this statement was allowed to pass unchallenged, Mr. Morley merely saying in a resigned sort of way, "He was certainly a brave soldier," and Corinna creating a diversion by jumping up and going to stand beside her cousin to show off her own pretty dress of tabby silk and the pearl pendant that 'Cousin Julian' had given her to mark the occasion, a piece of forward behaviour that earned her a sharp rebuke from a father who did not hold with young things, getting above themselves. It was left to the good-natured Johnnie to soothe her mortification, drawing her attention to some of the delicacies that composed the second course and supplying her with a heaped dish of fairy butter and some Naples biscuits, "Just as though I was quite grown up," she later confided to her mama.

Talk turned to the wedding journey. Julian was deliberately evasive, causing Aunt Sarah to wax sentimental over his obvious desire for solitude in which to enjoy wedded bliss, and Uncle William to remark with sour triumph that if he meant to take his wife gipsying about the country-side staying just where the fancy took them at this season of the year, he must be all about in his head. Since for once Julian found himself in entire agreement with the speaker, he could only be grateful when Anna came to his rescue, saying that it was time she changed her dress if they were to reach Town before the darkening, and adding that, although they would probably spend some days in Portman Square, they naturally did not wish this fact to be generally known. If the weather proved kind—and despite Uncle William's gloomy prognostications there *were* such things as crisp, clear January days—they might make one or two short excursions. In any case a message to Portman Square would soon catch up with them.

"And we might indeed spend tonight in Town," she repeated, as the coach bore them away at last. "I am rather tired and I daresay you are, too. I did not give Wayney a precise date, so she will not worry over our non-arrival, and it will be pleasanter to drive down to Bletchingley by daylight, as well as serving to pacify that absurdly tender conscience of yours."

He had to laugh, although the jibe about his conscience annoyed him. Men did not take to deceit so easily as females he thought, rather smugly. Moreover the lady's total lack of embarrassment in an unusual situation rankled slightly. She was, of course, relying upon his given word, as was only right and proper, but need she make it so very plain that she was interested only in the further-ance of her ridiculous schemes? The glamor-ous trappings of a long dead queen had dazzled him for a little while. He could still recall quite vividly the picture that his wife had presented as she showed them her gown, one hand holding out her spreading skirts, her head a little on one side so that the ringlets which had been carefully coaxed to fall from the intricate top-knot to frame her face had swung loosely about her throat. It was beau-tiful hair. The exact colour of the delicate golden circlet that had held her veil in place. He had felt proud of her. Proud of her self-possession, her poise and her intelligence.

Perhaps after all he had not done so badly for himself in the marriage stakes.

But the girl who sat beside him in the carriage, neat but unimpressive in her warm travelling mantle, was a very different creature from the glowing bride. There was nothing gentle and vulnerable about her to appeal to a man's protective instincts. She was a shrewd and competent campaigner, bent on her plan to dazzle society. He had a strong desire to ruffle that cool composure. A little teasing would not hurt her.

He said innocently. "What a fortunate circumstance that Miss Wayne should have chosen to retire to Bletchingley. It is scarcely an hour's drive from Pittsfield House."

She rose to the bait immediately. "But you are not to be taking advantage of that! You promised."

Julian hid his smile. *Not* so indifferent after all. "I did. And will keep my word. Though how I shall put on the time when I am obliged to skulk out of sight lest some mutual acquaintance sees me and wonders if I have made away with you, I really cannot imagine. You ought to have thought of that, you know."

She looked quite troubled. "I do see the difficulty," she admitted, "but I scarcely know what to suggest. You could hunt, I suppose. No one would think *that* odd, even when you are supposedly on your honeymoon. But if you stay in Town it is more difficult. Unless you have a taste for museums? You would not be likely to meet any of your friends there, would you?"

"But just imagine the comments if I *was* seen so engaged! Having apparently deserted my newly married wife in favour of a collection of dry-as-dust relics. I could not risk serving you such a back-handed turn."

The spontaneous gurgle of her laughter quite melted his heart. His vague sense of resentment fled and he hastened to reassure her the he would be perfectly adequately occupied during her absence. "I shall probably spend most of my time in Surrey," he added, "but I'll steer clear of Bletchingley. I shan't bother with the house—that will be for you to see to, with your father's assistance. But I mean to look into the working of the home farm. Some of my Uncle Thomas's notions were pretty mediaeval, and this is a good time of year to be thinking of new methods. And I daresay I shall manage a few days' hunting. That was a good notion of yours."

She mulled this over thoughtfully. "And if

A Marriage Arranged

Papa should suddenly descend on you it would be quite reasonable to explain that I had gone over to visit Wayney. Not that I think it at all likely."

She relapsed into silence. Absorbed in her plans and dreams, he thought amusedly, and heartily wished her well. His mind went back once more to the events of the day, to the picture she had presented in that beautiful, barbaric gown. He said slowly, "As your husband, whom you have just promised to honour and obey, may I make one humble request?"

She glanced up, startled out of her reverie, half amused by his solemn air.

"I understand that you mean to present the world with a new image of yourself," he went on. "Don't let fashionable notions change you too much. And promise me that you will not let any one cut your beautiful hair."

Eight

Two compliments on her wedding day. Three, really. For surely it was no small compliment that her husband should suggest that he did not want her to change too much. Painstakingly she brushed out her hair and studied it with new interest. It was just ordinary hair, she decided, unusual only in its luxuriance, absolutely straight with no hint of wave or curl, though it was docile enough, holding its shape for several hours if Cicely had used the irons on it. Perhaps it was the colour he had liked, a flat, even gold, neither red nor flaxen. That *was* rather out of the common, because her brows and lashes were dark.

She had need of all the comfort she could find in remembered compliments during the weeks she spent with Wayney. Only a fierce determination to prove that she could achieve what she had vowed to do held her to her strictly planned diet. Wayney had given it cautious approval and would willingly have shared the abstinence and the hunger pangs, but that, of course, Anna could not permit. So she was obliged to watch Wayney sustain nature on savoury stews and rich, mouth-watering pies while she must content herself with a wafer of chicken. It was all very well to say that she would not miss puddings and cakes since any way she did not care for them above half and much preferred fruit. But when one was so very hungry even the dullest of puddings looked tempting, and fruit, lacking the resources of the Wellasford succession houses, meant apples, already growing slightly wizened from storage.

Wayney, who had an excellent appetite and a figure like a hop pole, was almost as miserable as Anna. Fortunately the weather was clear and frosty, so they eventually solved the problem by taking their mid-day meal apart, Anna lunching first and then going off for a walk until Wayney had done.

By the end of the second week they were

both agreed that the wonderful plan was working. The thickening about the jaw-line, the fullness under the chin, were less pronounced, and Anna was sure that her dresses hung on her more loosely. Moreover she was becoming accustomed to the restricted diet, and was even able to turn up a virtuous nose at the delicious aroma of fresh-baked bread.

By the time the month was out, there could be no doubt about it. They were obliged to embark on the satisfactory task of taking in dresses to ensure a neat fit; and Anna, yielding to Wayney's urging to "eat a proper dinner for once" because it was the good soul's birthday, found herself unable to finish the hearty portion that she had accepted. Wayney was quite perturbed by this phenomenon, but Anna laughed and said it just showed that for years she had been eating far too much.

It was time to be thinking of a move to Town. A message was dispatched to Lord Wellasford setting a date some ten days ahead and asking that the carriage should be sent for her ladyship. His lordship having been obliged to go up to Town for a couple of nights, there was some small delay before his reply was received, but when eventually a groom brought the elegantly superscribed missive, her ladyship was gratified to learn that her husband proposed to do himself the honour of coming for her in person.

Miss Wayne, receiving this information with outward calm and inner excitement, said that she looked forward to meeting his lordship and suggested that they should see if they could finish the alterations to the green poplin with the quilted petticoat, but she was deeply shocked by Anna's sudden decision that her hair must be washed. Why! It was enough to give her her death. This was no time of year for washing one's hair, especially if one had such a quantity that it would take all day to dry.

Anna was apologetic but determined. She would put camomile flowers to steep overnight and wash it first thing in the morning. That would give it ample time to dry before his lordship's arrival. He had not mentioned a specific hour, but he would surely not be paying calls before mid-afternoon. Meanwhile, Wayney was quite right about the green poplin. With its white petticoat, lightly sprigged with yellow flowers, it seemed to speak of spring. Moreover it was a style that drew attention to a trim waist. Perhaps they could finish it tonight.

They did. Although it was past eleven when they sought their beds—very late by Wayney's

standards—and she also spoke strongly about
the extravagant use of working candles, delivering a little lecture on economical household
management which Anna accepted meekly,
quite understanding that it was just Wayney's
way of reasserting her authority after her
defeat on the topic of washing one's hair in
February.

In her belief that her husband would not be
paying calls at an unfashionably early hour,
however, Lady Wellasford was mistaken. Possibly he was thinking of the long drive back
to Town, or perhaps he was just curious to
discover how his bride had fared during their
separation. In either case he arrived shortly
after noon, catching the ladies drinking coffee after an early luncheon. His wife, who
had planned to astound him, not only by her
newly achieved slimness but by her generally soignée appearance, was attired in a
quilted petticoat with a wrapper about her
shoulders and her hair, almost dry, hanging
loose. Unfortunately Miss Wayne's elderly
maid, who was rather absent minded, remembered only that the gentleman was expected
and showed him directly into the parlour.

There was a startled silence. Anna's hands
flew up to pull the wrapper close about her
throat. To be sure, he was her husband. But

to catch her so in her petticoat! Miss Wayne rose, curtseying, her hand extended, an offer of refreshment on her lips.

His lordship was swift to perceive the embarrassment on both faces. He bowed politely to Miss Wayne, but addressed himself to his wife. "I see now why your father wanted you to wear your hair loose on our wedding day. How very right he was! I suppose I should apologise for arriving so early, but I refuse to say that I am sorry for a circumstance that has brought me so much pleasure."

The words could scarcely have been better chosen, and they were spoken with a half-laughing sincerity that carried conviction without being fulsome. Both ladies relaxed. Introductions were performed, and his lordship, declining wine, accepted the offer of a cup of coffee. Anna, going off to complete her toilet, was persuaded without difficulty to leave her hair loose a little longer, Miss Wayne obligingly reminding her of the pains and penalties consequent upon inadequate drying, and then settling down happily to make the acquaintance of dear Anna's husband, while fresh coffee was brewed.

An hour passed very pleasantly, his lordship drinking his coffee and commending the little queen cakes that Miss Wayne herself had

baked. Anna, having put on the green poplin
over-dress, sitting quietly by the fire, declining the queen cakes with a rueful twinkle at
Wayney, occasionally holding out a strand of
hair on the comb to help the drying process
and listening to the easy talk between the
other two. She was very well pleased with
life. It had all been worth while. Nothing had
been said but from time to time she had seen
her husband's thoughtful gaze bent upon her
and she knew him well enough to make a
pretty accurate guess at the mixture of surprise, speculation, even a slightly reluctant
admiration that coloured his attitude. Not
admiration for her *appearance,* she hastened
to admonish herself, but for her resolution.

Presently he broached the subject, saying
that he was relieved to find her looking so
well and expressing his gratitude to Miss
Wayne who must, he felt sure, have exerted
her restraining influence to keep the experi-
ment within reasonable bounds.

The ladies exchanged a little smile but
were not prepared to be drawn on this head.
His lordship said temperately, "I find you a
good deal changed, I must confess. But if you
can assure me that you have suffered no ill
effects I am content. No doubt I shall accus-
tom myself in time."

He could scarcely, supposed Anna, have proclaimed openly that he found her vastly improved! A little amused by the predicament in which he found himself, she took pity on him. "No ill effects at all, except on my temper," she told him with a twinkle. "Poor Wayney suffered dreadfully during the first weeks. I was the crossest thing in nature. But that is all over with now, and actually I feel very much better for my weeks of abstinence. In fact I have come to think that there may have been sound practical reasons for the old Lenten restrictions. Papa, I know, holds that many such practices have their roots in common sense and a knowledge of the behaviour that is conducive to good health. Like not eating pig meat in hot countries where pigs are scavengers," she explained sagely.

"Then I profoundly trust that you can persuade him to accept that explanation when he enquires why I have been starving his daughter," suggested Julian with a rueful grimace.

For a moment she looked both startled and penitent, but she was swift to make a recovery. "He won't notice if I wear my old loose gowns," she declared triumphantly, "and he was always opposed to tight lacing."

He looked dubious, and delighted her by

saying, "It's not just the gowns. Your face looks quite different. It is not so round. And your neck looks longer, while as for your eyes, they look bigger than ever." And I never realised how long and dark your lashes were, he might have added, save that he was deliberately keeping this very personal exchange on a prosaic footing. "I should think he is bound to notice. But we shall see."

The ladies excused themselves presently, Wayney offering to help Anna put up her hair and finish her packing. They were not long gone, and when they came down to the parlour again Anna mentioned her desire to see Pittsfield House. "It seems only sensible when we are so near. Then we can begin planning what needs to be done. Do you think we might spend tonight there? We need not hurry ourselves—tomorrow will do perfectly well for our return to Town."

Julian raised no objection to this suggestion, save to remind her that Pittsfield House was pretty bleak and comfortless but that he dared say they would take little hurt by staying the night in it.

Anna's farewell to Wayney was brief, for it would not be long, she promised, before they met again. "You must come and help us with the house, when Papa and I set to work in earnest," she said gaily, and informed Julian that Wayney had an excellent eye for colour. "Only first I must buy a great many clothes," she stipulated, as Julian wrapped her cloak about her, surveying that sober garment with disfavour.

During the short drive from Bletchingley she enquired in very wifely fashion about his progress with his farming problems, some of her questions so sensible and pertinent that he eventually expressed surprise that a female should have so intelligent a grasp of what was usually regarded as a masculine province.

He was the first personable young man with whom she had enjoyed a friendly relationship. To pursue that relationship, even to the verge of flirtation, with the added savour of knowing that the gentleman was her husband, was a new and delightful pastime. If she had spoken truth she could have told him that she would have displayed equal interest in Mr. Arkwright's spinning machine or Crompton's mule—had *his* interests lain in that direction. Instead she said demurely, "I do my best to understand such things, milord. Papa has always impressed upon me that all sound commercial enterprise must be based upon a healthy agricultural policy. His exposition frequently took me out of my depth, but even I could see that every one needs to eat, whether they toil in these vast new mills and manufactories or travel overseas to sell the goods produced."

Very naturally it was Julian's pleasure to explain these mysteries a little more fully to so intelligent and receptive a pupil.

In the failing light it was not possible to make a detailed inspection of Pittsfield House, but Anna saw enough to realise that Julian had not exaggerated the Spartan nature of the accommodation. The bones of the house were beautiful but a good deal needed to be done if she wanted to enjoy the standard of comfort to which she was accustomed. Draughts abounded. Food had to be carried so far from the kitchens that it must inevitably be cold upon its arrival at table, and all water had to be drawn from a pump in the stable yard. Fortunately there was one thing that she could praise without reserve, for none of the chimneys smoked, not even the one in her bedchamber where a fire had been hastily kindled.

Over dinner Julian told her about his trip to Town. He had driven up to obtain some publications that dealt with the selective breeding of cattle, and while in Portman

Square had been startled to receive a call from Lady Holroyd, who had chanced to see him in the street and had impulsively decided that it was high time that she called upon her new tenants, naturally supposing (she said) that his bride would be in Town with him, so newly wed as they were. She had been disappointed, of course, but had sent all kinds of welcoming messages—well, no, he couldn't remember exactly what they were, but all about being great friends, just like the old days, and about Anna being sure to let her know as soon as she was fixed in Town. Oh yes! And she had made rather a fuss about one of the pictures that they had stored away.

"Seems it was a portrait of the late Sir Marmaduke. She couldn't bear to take him into that pokey little hole in North Audley Street—her description, not mine—so she left him in surroundings more appropriate to his dignity. Apparently the thought that *we* had packed him off to the attics was exceedingly painful, so if you will have him looked out she will dispatch him to their country place where, presumably, he will be able to rest in peace. Just like Caro in one of her fusses. It was always easiest to let her have her own way. Though I wouldn't mind laying you odds that by the time we reach Town she'll have forgotten all about it. 'Fraid I played along with her. The thing is, I thought I'd better turn her up sweet because I thought she might be a useful friend for you—knows everyone who *is* anyone and can recommend you to the most fashionable dressmakers and milliners."

It was thoughtful of him, and Anna had no desire to be disobliging. She had taken a sincere liking to Johnnie Merridew and this was his sister. But for one reason or another she felt no great eagerness to be 'great friends' with Lady Holroyd. Even from Julian's half laughing account she sounded spoilt and pettish, while as for the ridiculous fuss about her husband's portrait, it was just the sort of whim that a spoiled beauty would invent in order to centre attention on herself. If she had cared so much she would never have left the portrait in the hands of strangers. There was the rub, of course. Julian was not a stranger. And that was another odd thing. She, Anna, had not been a wife for very long. Some people might even say that she was not a wife at all. But already she found herself resenting Lady Holroyd's calm appropriation of Julian. So they would all be great friends would they? Just like old times. Well—there could be two opinions about that.

She said pleasantly, "I don't doubt she would be able to help me in any number of ways. We must certainly invite her to our parties— unless you think it might distress her to attend parties in the house that she shared with her husband. But I do not mean to tax her kindness by burdening her with all my small social problems. I am sure she would find it a dead bore, even if she was too polite to say so. As for clothes"—she broke into a gleeful chuckle—"no one, but *no one*, not even the Queen's own dresser, shall lay a meddling finger on those."

She put both elbows on the table and rested her chin on her clasped hands, smiling across at him in frank comradeship and looking, though she was quite unaware of it, distinctly delectable.

"I warned you of *some* of my odd notions," she reminded him, "but I dared not tell you the full score lest you should cry off. You were my only chance, you see, and I *could* not take such a risk." The mischief in face and voice, the mock penitence in the pose of the down-bent head, were a challenge that he found difficult to resist. He was aware of a strong desire to kiss the laughing, teasing

mouth. But this new Anna was a stranger—
and, he suspected, a shy, wary creature that
must be coaxed and gentled before it would
endure a caress.

"So?" he asked amusedly.

She looked down thoughtfully at her clasped
hands. "I know exactly what I want to do,"
she said simply. "Exactly what suits my
colouring, how far to follow fashion, when to
risk a daring originality. I think I have studied every fashion magazine that has been
published in this country these two years
past, and a number of French ones as well. I
know all the mercers who supplied Papa with
the materials for his collection and have already chosen a number of lengths suited to
my needs. I shall buy more when we reach
Town. Meanwhile Cicely and the sewing maids
are already at work on my new dresses. I
could not endure to reach London after all
this time only to have to stay indoors because
I had nothing to wear. So *that* is all smoothly
arranged. But there are two things on which
I would like your advice."

Julian supposed that he should have expected efficiency in organisation from one
whose training had been supervised by Mr.
Morley, but he had not in fact done so. He
was therefore thankful to discover that the

first problem was simple enough. Even in London one must have fresh air and exercise. But gentle strolls in the Park and decorous expeditions to the shops held small appeal for the country bred Anna. She already rode— rather well, she told him, with that calm evaluation of her various talents and failings that he was beginning to accept as characteristic—but astride. Would her husband advise her to learn to ride side-saddle, or to drive— perhaps a phaeton?

"Both," returned Julian promptly. "We are not just thinking of this one Season, remember, but of our whole lives. Perhaps you may not always wish to spend the whole of the spring and summer in Town, but you are bound to want to come up from time to time for shopping and the theatres and to parties. Once we have our own house it will be simple enough, but when we are in Town we must subscribe to Town notions. If you already ride pretty well you will soon adapt to the side-saddle. To be honest, I agree with your father that side-saddles are an invention of the Devil. But in this case the Devil must be served, for you cannot ride astride in a London park. Fortunately you are not permitted to gallop, either, and with a little practice you will soon achieve a creditable canter. I will charge myself with the responsibility of acquiring a mount that is accustomed to carrying a lady without being totally lacking in character and paces. Also a phaeton and pair warranted to take the wind out of the eye of any other lady with social aspirations that match your own."

She nodded gratefully. "It sounds horrid when you put it bluntly like that, but it is precisely what I meant. And perhaps you could put me in the way of handling the reins in form? For I have never driven a pair."

"It's a pity that this place is so uncomfortable," said Julian reflectively. "These arts would have been better acquired in the seclusion of the country. But I daresay you will be wanting to take dancing lessons, too, and for those you will *have* to return to Town. Well," as she nodded, "there is no help for it then. We shall just have to get up very early so that you can practise before the rest of the world is astir. This promises to be an uncommonly strenuous Season! What was your other problem?"

"You mentioned dancing lessons," she said slowly. "And I have been planning all kinds of parties, from informal breakfasts to a grand ball. But has it occurred to you that we might find our rooms remarkably thin of company?

Neither of us has a wide acquaintance to draw upon. We shall make friends gradually, no doubt, but I don't think people will call as they do in the country. Especially as we are only hiring the house."

It was a difficulty that had not occurred to him but he could see that it was a real one. He rubbed his jaw thoughtfully with one knuckle, but no immediate solution came to mind.

His wife said tentatively, "Would you permit me to engage a—a sort of companion, I suppose is the best description? The thing is, I had already engaged her to come in daily as my secretary. I thought there could be no objection to *that*, because I shall need someone, you know, to deal with all the arrangements for our parties. But now I think it would be better if she came to live with us, and came as soon as she is free to do so."

Fortunately Julian was a tolerant creature. He supposed, with a hidden grin, that he should be thankful to be consulted at all for there seemed to be a good deal of decision about his wife at the moment.

"Tell me about her," he invited.

With that unexpected sensitivity to what he was thinking rather than what he had actually said, she prefaced her account with an awkward apology.

"I'm sorry that I should appear to be such a managing female. I suppose Papa has spoiled me, permitting me to have far too much of my own way, and I have not yet grown accustomed to being married and having someone else to consider. But at least I would not invite anyone to come and live in your house without consulting you."

"*Our* house," he smiled at her. "And I will undertake to do as much for you. But I am consumed with curiosity. Who *is* this social oracle? And why have I not heard of her before?"

The meeting had been accidental, it emerged, Mrs. Kingston having slipped and twisted her ankle on the steps of the theatre just as Aunt Sarah and Anna were descending them to the waiting carriage. They had conveyed her to her home in Hill Street and that would have been the end of it, but Aunt Sarah had decided that they should call next day to enquire how the sufferer did. Hill Street, she explained, was not only fashionable but exclusive. Mrs. Kingston, for all her plain dress and lack of jewellery, had the air of one born to the purple. Aunt Sarah might have been moved, in emergency, by her natural kindly instincts. Further consideration had suggested to her that Mrs. Kingston's accident might prove downright providential. How if it were to give her that entrée to the world of the well-born which she had sought so long?

But the visit had proved disappointing. Mrs. Kingston—the Honourable Mrs. Kingston—was certainly well connected. So much Aunt Sarah had been able to discover by diligent enquiry. But she was a widow in straitened circumstances and had largely withdrawn from society. Her father had dissipated a fortune that was never more than moderate long before she made her début and had been thankful to dispose of his three daughters to any respectable suitors who offered. Margaret had been fortunate. She had been permitted to marry a childhood friend, a hopelessly ineligible younger son, with whom she had shared five years of cheerful hand-to-mouth existence before he had been killed in a fall from a half-broke horse that he was schooling.

"I had one stroke of good fortune," she had told Anna, much later in their acquaintance. "Christopher's Godmother"—Christopher was her husband—"had taken a liking to me. She invited me to make my home here with her, and when she died she left me the house and a tiny annuity. It is scarcely sufficient to keep the place up, but I have found one or two means of adding to it."

Aunt Sarah had abandoned this blind alley after her first visit. Anna, with time on her hands and attracted by the quiet charm of the woman who had emerged in such a pleasant guise from the buffetings of fate, had called again, to leave a nosegay of flowers and offer to exchange library books while the injured ankle was still painful. She had been kindly received, and gradually an undemanding friendship had grown up between the pair. When Anna went home they had kept up a correspondence. That was how the girl had learned that Mrs. Kingston occasionally took charge of débutantes who had no relative in a position to do so, introducing them into Society and, in certain cases, arranging for presentation at Court.

"She wrote the most delightful letters," Anna went on. "Full of comical tales of her various charges but affectionate and understanding, too. And I know her and like her. I thought she would be just the person to advise me about entertaining, because it will be quite different from acting hostess for Papa. *His* guests were either business acquaintances or friends who shared his interest in antiquities. All I had to do was house them comfortably and feed them well. When it comes to planning parties with music or dancing or cards, I am an absolute ignoramus. Only now it is a little more than that. Who is to come to our parties? If Margaret were to live with us for a little while she could take me about as she did her débutantes, so that I should meet people. That would be a beginning. And I daresay you will make new acquaintances at your club." She chuckled unexpectedly. "Margaret says there will be no difficulty in filling our rooms with young gentlemen. Since we are newly wed and there are no marriageable daughters on the catch for them we have only to provide good wine and excellent refreshments and they will be perfectly happy to seek refuge with us."

The shrewd good humour of this comment appealed to him. He began to think quite favourably of Mrs. Kingston. Undoubtedly Anna needed someone with experience to advise and support her, and if she preferred paid help to the casual services of Caro Holroyd, she should have it. It might work out pretty well. Come to think of it, he was not at all sure that he wanted Caro in and out of the house for ever. He had found her slightly embarrassing, with her huge, yearning eyes and her gentle hints at the great love that had linked them in the past. Star-crossed, she had sighed. And it was no such thing. He could recall the whole business perfectly clearly, and admittedly, at seventeen, he had been tail over top in love with her ethereal prettiness. She had been very lovely. But he could remember just as clearly the way that she had laughed at him when he had begged her to wait. To wait until he could persuade his father to let him take over the home farm and turn it into a profitable concern.

"I suppose you think that I could milk the cows and feed the pigs. Churn the butter, too, I make no doubt. Perhaps even sell eggs in the market."

A stripling of seventeen did not fall out of love with his idol for one shrewish speech, but he had been sadly disillusioned that their ideas should be so far apart. At least it had in some sort prepared him for the day when she had broken to him the news that she was to marry Sir Marmaduke Holroyd. A decent enough fellow, by all accounts, but old enough to be her father.

"He can give me a house in Town and pretty dresses and horses and a carriage. Jewels, too," she had sighed contentedly. "I am sorry for it, Julian, but after all it would never have done. You are younger than I. Close on two years, which is a great deal when it is the wrong way round."

He wondered how she would like it if he were to remind her of that speech now. 'Star-crossed', indeed!

He accorded Anna's tentative suggestion his sincere approval with an enthusiasm that quite surprised her.

Nine

Anna's long-planned program moved smoothly into action. Housekeeping presented no difficulties, though the variety of tempting viands presented by the London provision merchants was something of a trial to a young lady who was watching her figure. Bailey—the butler—and Mrs. Ellis were competent and seemed to have established harmonious relations with their underlings, and there could be no denying that Lady Holroyd's house was equipped with every modern convenience. The kitchen boasted an enclosed stove, which not only provided vastly improved cooking and baking facilities but also heated water. There was even a bathroom. To be sure the water supply was temperamental, varying from a trickle to a gush, and hot water must, of course, be laboriously carried from the kitchen. But it was a great luxury, as was the indoor closet, which enjoyed the distinction of being flushed out by that same temperamental water supply.

For the first week of their sojourn the sewing room was a hive of industry. A number of dresses were almost finished, requiring only the final adjustments that would ensure a perfect fit. The capacious cupboards in Lady Wellasford's room filled steadily.

Margaret Kingston was their first caller, coming in response to a note from Anna announcing their arrival in Town. From the start, Julian was inclined to like her and to think that his wife had chosen wisely. She was plainly but fashionably dressed and had a quiet air of assurance. Probably in her early forties, he judged. She wasted no time in polite small talk but began at once to suggest various ways in which they could meet people.

"I shall take you calling with me," she told Anna, "and we can drive together in the Park. What kind of carriage do you keep, and do you propose to drive yourself?"

They discussed this from every aspect and finally decided that it would be best to use the landau with the coachman to drive the two ladies. "In state," pronounced Mrs. Kingston cheerfully. "And I'll not pretend it won't be a treat for me, as well as a good way of introducing you informally to my friends. You've no idea how much you miss the comfort of having your own carriage until you've had to depend on hirelings," she told Julian. "In fact I will frankly confess that I am looking forward to spending a few months in the lap of luxury. I can think of nothing more delightful than to enjoy all the pleasures of the Season in supreme comfort and delightful company. I shall feel positively guilty in accepting the handsome salary that your wife insists upon paying me. It seems wrong to be paid for such pleasant service. But I *can* be helpful over all the tiresome details of entertaining, and I *can* introduce her to a number of pleasant people. I promise you, milord, that I will take good care of her and do my utmost to promote her interests."

Yes, confirmed Julian. He liked her very well. She was straightforward and unaffected. It would be no penance to have her living under his roof. It might even help to ease the occasional awkwardness of being married and yet not married. This had already cropped up in the business of allocating bedchambers. Mrs. Ellis had naturally caused the principal suite of rooms to be prepared. Unfortunately it consisted of one large bedroom with two dressing rooms opening off it—and these could only be reached by passing through the bedroom. Julian had hastily made up a tale about the dressing rooms being too small. His wife would need them both to accommodate the quantity of clothes that she intended to buy. He himself would occupy one of the guest-rooms, across the corridor from his wife, which had its own slightly larger dressing room. He had tried to make this lame story sound jocular and light-hearted, and Mrs. Ellis had not blinked an eye-lash, but he still felt hot under the collar when he recalled the incident. Give Anna her due. She had expressed penitence for having overlooked the possibility of such a situation arising and begged his pardon very prettily.

They discussed arrangements for a card party and a musical soirée to be held as soon as possible and a fairly large rout party to take place before the set ball, which Mrs. Kingston advised them to defer until after Anna's presentation. Then Anna carried her friend off to look at her new dresses and to decide which of the rooms she would prefer for her personal use. Margaret had outstanding engagements which would prevent her from moving in with them for one or two days, but was quite ready to embark on a round of morning calls, taking Anna with her, on the very next day.

Time flew. Mrs. Kingston was indefatigable. Julian found himself escorting the ladies to a play or a concert, accompanying them on a strolling shopping expedition, where they did not seem to buy very much but met and chatted with a great many other ladies similarly employed. Meekly he sought out former acquaintances from his school and army days, some of whom he could scarcely remember, and suggested that they should bring their wives to call on his. An old friend of his mother's, met by chance at Tattersall's, took a kindly interest in him and volunteered to put his name up for Boodles and Almack's, an offer which he accepted with becoming gratitude though he had little taste for games of chance. Like his wife he came to know a great many people by name, though there was scant opportunity for acquaintance to ripen into friendship. The reception rooms of his London house were no longer thin of company. And Julian was beginning to wish that he had never hired the place. For Caro Holroyd haunted it. Naturally they invited her to all their parties, and inevitably she accepted. Perhaps, it was equally inevitable that she and Anna should take an instant dislike to one another. Anna was coolly courteous. Caro—when Julian was at hand—was all wide-eyed admiration for the changes that Anna's artistic taste had wrought in her former home. When he was not, her manner could only be described as insolent. In some subtle feminine fashion she managed to convey to her fellow guests the impression that she was especially privileged. She assumed the airs of a hostess, pressing them to partake of this or that delicacy, directing their activities as though this was still her house and it was her hospitality that they were enjoying.

Margaret Kingston was outspokenly indignant. "I'm just waiting for her to coax *me* into accepting a piece of cook's special Nun's cake, with her deprecating smile and her big beseeching eyes and her assurance that the recipe has been in her family for generations, and I shall ask her how it comes that nuns have families. I will! I vow to do it."

Anna had to laugh, even though she shared Margaret's anger. "It is she who loses dignity," she said soothingly. "You must have seen how people look at her a little sideways, trying to work out where she fits into the family. I have yet to see one succumb whole-heartedly to her wiles."

"Little she cares for surprised faces and sideways glances so long as she is in the centre of the picture," retorted Margaret. As for succumbing to her wiles, she thought savagely, you need look no further than your husband. For as far as she could see, Lord Wellasford was wholly hoodwinked. He accepted Lady Holroyd's outrageous demands on his time and attention without complaint, appeared to find her quite charming, and was at some pains to ensure that she was never neglected.

As Julian had prophesied, his wife had taken readily to the side-saddle and presented a charming picture in her severe dark green habit. She admitted that she did not feel quite so secure as when riding astride, but pointed out without a blush that she certainly looked a good deal more elegant. Learning to drive took rather longer. Her teacher was strict, the time at their disposal limited. Once or twice he took her out to Richmond where he could hand over the reins with the reasonable assurance that they would not be overlooked by any of their new acquaintances, and it was on her return from one such afternoon excursion that she found the usually even-tempered Margaret awaiting her in a positive fury of wrath.

"That woman!" she almost spat. "That insinuating snake! I am deeply sorry for it and feel that I have been shockingly at fault, but indeed I could never have guessed what she meant to do. You had not been gone above an hour when she was announced. Quite distracted, she informs me, because she has lost a locket that held a portrait of her husband. I assured her that nothing of the kind has been found here and that the servants are perfectly to be trusted. She apologises for disturbing me—I was writing the invitations for the ball—and will see herself out. That was where I made my mistake. Disliking her as I do, I was in no mood to show her any excessive civility, so I let her do so and went on with my work. Some little time later in comes Mrs. Ellis, very much ruffled, wishing to know if she is to order a room to be prepared for Lady Holroyd, she having found her ladyship strolling about upstairs apparently inspecting the bedroom accommodation. As you may guess I was absolutely furious and would have told the wretch precisely what I thought of her vulgar curiosity, but by the time I reached the hall she was on the point of departure and Bailey was there listening to every word. Her ladyship all sweet dissemblance, of course. She was so sorry. Had just stepped upstairs to look for her locket, not wishing to be a trouble to any one. And in searching for it and in admiring the charming decorative schemes, she had not realised how the time had sped. I am ashamed to have let myself be gulled so easily—but who could have dreamed that a woman of breeding would sink so low?"

Anna felt a little sick. She had come hurrying in happily, eager to tell Margaret that she had been learning how to loop a rein and had actually earned one or two words of praise. Now the happy mood was blighted, the bubbling words died on her lips. There was something peculiarly distasteful in the thought of an intruder wandering at will through her private apartments. Nor could she set Lady Holroyd's behaviour down to idle curiosity. The lady's malice had been shown too plainly for that. She did not know quite what she feared but she shivered a little and for a moment her usual easy poise was shaken so that she said bitterly, "Not being a woman of breeding myself, I am scarcely qualified to judge."

She repented at once, seeing the hurt in Margaret's face, swiftly as it was controlled, and putting out one hand in a gesture of appeal. "That was horrid of me. No need to rip up at you, just because I have allowed that woman's actions to cut up my peace of mind. It is my turn to beg pardon, and indeed I do. And of course you could not guess what she intended. No woman of principle would behave so, be she gentle or simple."

The subject was allowed to drop and they reverted to discussion of the arrangements for the rout party. But the shadow of unease was not wholly lifted from Anna's mind and she began to pay more attention to Lady Holroyd's unpleasant skirmishings. She could not imagine what the woman hoped to gain by being actively unpleasant and could only suppose that her ladyship found it galling to see another playing hostess—and very successfully, too—in the rooms where she had always been queen. How could she guess that Lady Holroyd, having exercised her prying instincts to the full, had gone away full of curiosity about the domestic harmony of the Wellasfords? She found it very odd that a couple so recently married should occupy separate apartments. Admittedly only a corridor separated them—but still! She gave the matter a good deal of thought.

She was no more in love with Julian than she had been when he had made her the object of his clumsy calf-love years before, but she hated the thought that another woman had snapped him up now, when he had inherited the title and his uncle's fortune as well. If only *she* had met him first! It was easy to see that he had only married this stolid provincial in order to regain Wellasford, and she rather thought that *her* charms would have outweighed the appeal of a fusty old house. As a frail, pathetic widow it should not have been a difficult task to re-animate his feelings towards her. He had always fallen an easy prey to any call upon his chivalry and in that respect he did not seem to have altered very much. She could twist him round her finger with no difficulty at all. How infuriating, then, that he should have married just before they met again. However, there might still be some amusements to be found in trying if one could drive a rift in the marriage. It would be something of a triumph to attach Julian, his honeymoon scarce finished, to her train of admirers, and it would give her considerable satisfaction to lower the crest of the girl who was bidding fair to be London's latest toast. She set herself to devise one or two pinpricks which should spoil young Lady Wellasford's pleasure in the approaching rout party.

These did not succeed quite as well as she had hoped. Anna, having now taken the lady's measure, was more than a match for petty spite. When Lady Holroyd, having carefully waited until her hostess was within ear-shot, informed her companions, "Oh, yes. I suppose one might call her handsome. And I will allow that her hair is natural. But I would swear that she darkens her eyebrows," Anna made no pretence of not having heard. She joined the little group with her friendliest smile, passed a handkerchief over the maligned eyebrows and held it out for their inspection, saying on a note of apology, "Actually you are mistaken, ma'am. But I assure you that I would not hesitate to do so if I thought it was necessary. Why not? After all, a great many older ladies use such arts to restore a youthful glow to fading locks." Which caused one or two of the group to look remarkably wooden-faced, while one surprised maiden emitted a nervous giggle. Lady Holroyd coloured angrily. The delicate tinting of her hair cost her a pretty penny and she had not thought that any one was privy to her secret.

Perhaps this reverse clouded her judgment, so that in her next essay she blundered badly. She found herself in converse with an elderly dame who was unknown to her, but whose easy arrogance undoubtedly denoted the bluest of blue blood. In such company she was usually at her most innocent and insinuating, rarely delivering herself of any definite opinion lest it clash with the views of her companion. But when the lady chose to comment on the Wellasford marriage, she allowed ill humour to lead her into error. 'An unusual match' the lady had called it. "Do you think so, ma'am?" returned Lady Holroyd with an angry titter. "I would call it commonplace enough. An arranged marriage—birth and title on one side, wealth on the other."

The stranger turned her head to look at her in regal fashion, raising a glass that hung at her bosom to do so the more impressively. "Indeed!" she said gently. "An interesting view. Though I should have thought that Wellasford had no need to hang out for a rich bride. Not, in any case, since he inherited his uncle's fortune. While as for the bride, she appears to me both well-bred and well-mannered, which is more than one can say for some of her guests. Personally I am in favour of arranged marriages, provided there is no great inequality in age or fortune. I look forward to closer acquaintance with Lady Wellasford. No doubt I shall meet her frequently at Almack's."

It was a crushing rebuff. The real sting lay in that final sentence. Lady Holroyd had never been admitted to that exclusive gathering that was gradually becoming known as the Marriage Mart. Her own birth was no more than respectable, and although she had expected her marriage to Sir Marmaduke to admit her to the inner circles of the 'ton', her expectations had not been fulfilled. Sir Marmaduke was an easy-going, middle-aged gentleman, more addicted to the pleasures of the table and the vine than to the observation of social niceties. He did not so much *resist* his wife's efforts to bring the pair of them into fashionable prominence as permit them to slide over him. He was a kind husband, but no efforts of hers could turn him into one of the smarts.

The discovery that the elderly lady was none other than Lady Penmarston, one of society's most formidable dowagers and quite the most exclusive hostess in Town, did nothing to lessen her discomfiture.

"Oh! *That* fusty old thing," she said, with a would-be indifferent shrug. But very soon afterwards she decided that she was developing the headache, and excusing herself to her hostess with a brusqueness that was barely courteous, had her carriage summoned to bear her back to North Audley Street, there to lick her wounds and plan anew.

Ten

If Anna cherished the hope that the encounter at the rout party would persuade Lady Holroyd to keep a respectful distance, she was sadly disappointed. The unwelcome guest haunted the house more assiduously than ever, until her reluctant hostess's courtesy was sorely strained and she admitted to Margaret that she was almost tempted to instruct Bailey to deny her.

"But how can I, when she and my husband are such old friends?" she said resignedly.

"And the lady as sweet as honey when *he* is within hearing," rejoined Margaret tartly. "No. It does make things difficult. Frankly I abominate the woman. But I do not see that she can do you any harm, however willing she may be. Jealous of your success, I must suppose. But do not under-rate her. She would serve you a back-handed trick if she could."

Anna concurred. Privately she thought there was a little more to it than jealousy—at least jealousy of social success—though no doubt that added substantially to Lady Holroyd's dislike. For Anna's success was more marked with every passing day. Thanks to Margaret's unofficial sponsorship she met all the right people. Thanks to her own straightforward simplicity and total lack of pretension she was accepted for what she was—a pleasant-mannered girl of good disposition, wealthy and well-educated if not well-born. Gradually her sincerity and her natural warmth had their effect. Acceptance blossomed into liking, so that she felt she had a number of real friends, even if they *were* of recent standing. As for admiration, even adulation, she had that in full measure. If she had taken all the compliments that were showered upon her at their face value she might well have become intolerably conceited. Fortunately her own good sense and Margaret's dry comments convinced her that the whole thing was no more than an air-ball, growing with every heedless breath and just as easily deflated. If one gentleman chose to praise her lovely hair or her graceful carriage, his friends would immediately strive to out-do him in graceful metaphor. Dozens of posies were sent to her, poems were written in her praise, the house was besieged by morning callers and two young gentlemen almost came to fisticuffs in the ballroom because one vowed that the other had claimed the dance that Lady Wellasford had promised to him.

Margaret's lighthearted prophecies about the popularity of the Wellasfords with the younger gentlemen had been amply fulfilled. They flocked about this charming new hostess, and after a little initial shyness Anna found them, in general, very likeable. She was rather older than most of them and, since she was married, no one could suspect her of being on the catch for them. So she was able to be her natural self. She chuckled over their various escapades, sympathised with their disappointments and occasionally scolded them for reckless folly. In short, as one admiring young reprobate confided to a select group of his cronies, "She's just like the best kind of sister, only prettier and more amusing and far more interested in our affairs."

As Margaret had predicted they ate her

excellent refreshments and drank perhaps more of her wine than was quite desirable, but they had their own code of conduct and in return she was never without a band of attentive escorts to supply her least want wherever she went. It might be no more than the provision of a glass of lemonade or the summoning of her carriage when she wished to leave a party early, but it gave her the sense of being cossetted and cared for. Behind the occasionally clumsy gallantries, the rather laboured compliments, lay a genuine if mild affection, and the girl who had never enjoyed the comradeship of brothers and sisters revelled in the easy, undemanding society of these youngsters.

She was well liked, too, by her own sex, a much more difficult achievement. Her own disastrous first season gave her an insight into the difficulties of the callow fledglings and she was able to help some of the more nondescript girls in a number of unobtrusive ways, thus earning their passionate gratitude and, incidentally, that of their mothers. By the time of her presentation at Court even the haughtiest of dames allowed her to be quite a pretty-behaved female, and there was a general feeling that young Wellasford had done very well for himself.

The presentation passed off smoothly enough. Privately Julian thought that his wife looked magnificent; a good deal more regal than any of the royalties to whom she made her successive curtseys. Hoops were still de rigueur at Court and Anna had been glad of her new slenderness as she watched the great white bell of her skirt swing out from the tiny waist. On Margaret's advice she had chosen to wear white, and her husband, much pleased with his own knowledgeableness, had exclaimed, upon seeing it, "Samite!"

"Specially woven?" he enquired next.

Anna nodded. "And shockingly expensive, too," she confided ruefully. "But I meant to wear it for our own ball, so you mustn't scold me too harshly for extravagance."

"I don't care *what* it cost," declared Julian largely. "It is worth every penny to see you look so becomingly. And that is the Roman necklet that you wore at dinner the first time we met," he finished triumphantly. "Nothing could sort better with the fabric of your gown."

Anna blushed to the tips of her ears and murmured something slightly incoherent about fine feathers. It was an odd thing. In the general way compliments no longer set her heart fluttering, but her husband's praise was very sweet. Perhaps it was because she had had her fill of well-turned phrases. Julian was neither glib nor particularly fluent, but he always sounded entirely sincere. Maybe *that* was why his rare praise stirred her pulses where the smoothly worded admiration of others left her with no more than a mild satisfaction.

She pulled herself together to explain that Papa had travelled up to Town especially to bring her the necklace and to see her in all her Court finery. He and Margaret were to have a quiet dinner together. On the day after that memorable rout party Lady Penmarston had come to pay a formal call, in the course of which she had most obligingly offered to present the bride. Margaret had strongly recommended acceptance of such a distinguishing attention.

"Nothing could be better," she had said at once. "Yes, of course *I could* do it, as we had arranged, but I would not put it beyond your dear friend Lady Holroyd to set it about that I had been well paid for the undertaking. Oh! I would willingly forego a month's salary for a sight of her face when she hears that Lady Penmarston is your sponsor."

She was not, rather naturally, granted that privilege, and by the time that Lady Holroyd put in an appearance at the Wellasfords' ball, she had presumably swallowed any feelings of chagrin, for she was at her sweetest—even to Anna—and in quite her best looks. She had put off her blacks some weeks before, and on this notable occasion there was no pretence of even half mourning. Her dress was an ethereal creation of finest guaze in shades of blue and green, and with pearls about her throat and twisted among her fair curls she looked like some sea nymph who had strayed from her natural element, the wistful, heart-shaped face somehow conveying the impression that she sought a warm human love. It was a little unfortunate that Anna should chance to overhear her husband gallantly informing the lady the she did not look a day older than she had done on her seventeenth birthday, and that her gown put him strongly in mind of the one that she had worn on that occasion. A harmless courtesy. How was Anna to know how skillfully its recipient had angled for the compliment, nor how carefully she had directed her strolling progress with her host to a point where his wife could not help but hear? She knew that it was foolish to refine too much upon so trivial an incident, but it slightly dashed her pleasure in an otherwise highly successful function. Nor did she feel much enthusiasm as she seconded her husband's acceptance of Lady Holroyd's invitation to dinner on the following Thursday.

"Just a small party, I am afraid. One simply cannot *move* if there are more than eight people in the room. But Sir Aubrey Drysdale is so anxious to meet the latest belle. Quite a connoisseur, you know, and perfectly unexceptionable. Not the most rigid of husbands could take exception to his making you the object of his admiration. He is much too great a gentleman to go beyond the line. It is really a great compliment that he should be so eager to meet you."

This singularly inept speech restored Anna's good humour. It struck her as amusing that any one could be so clumsy even when obviously trying to be pleasant. She wondered if the gleam in Julian's eye meant that he shared her view, but he made no further reference to the invitation or its giver.

Margaret, however, had a good deal to say, especially about Sir Aubrey Drysdale. "Turning you up sweet," she remarked, with a regrettable lack of regard for elegant diction. "He's quite a catch. Never made one of *her* court, though I daresay he would be pretty well acquainted with her husband. Now why should she wish to thrust him upon *your* notice? I'd not trust that woman if she offered me the Crown Jewels and said the King himself had sent her. Up to mischief of some kind, you may be sure. But as for Sir Aubrey, he *is* pretty well what she said. A bit of a stick, to my way of thinking, but undoubtedly a paragon of perfection. Well-born, wealthy, handsome. A leader of fashion but not given to ridiculous extremes. Does everything well—rides—drives—fences—shoots. I don't know if he boxes, but if he does I am sure he does it neatly and with admirable discretion."

Anna gave a crack of laughter, "Heaven forefend that you should ever favour any one with a description of *me*," she exclaimed. "Not a word of dispraise have you uttered, but the picture you have painted is devastating. The man is a self satisfied prig."

But Margaret was quite serious. "Then I have done him an injustice," she said. "He has considerable charm of manner and is thought to be an asset to any kind of party, being reliable, punctual and punctilious in all the small courtesies that help to smooth the paths of social intercourse."

"Good gracious! A paragon indeed. I can scarcely wait to meet him in the flesh. Has he no faults?"

Margaret considered her reply carefully. "Not faults," she said fairly. "One foible— that made me take him on mild dislike. He shuns the society of single females, preferring that of married ladies. Perhaps one should not blame him too much. Ever since he was thrown upon the town he has been much harassed and hunted. I daresay he has been subjected to every device and trap known to a matchmaking mama. But—I am sorry for it—it is sheer prejudice—it still seems unnatural to me for a man of his age—and he must be all of five and thirty—to prefer the role of cicisbeo to the normal paths of courtship, betrothal and marriage. It is not as though he was the victim of a consuming passion for one particular female who had married some one else. In such a case one would be obliged to feel some compassion. But no, it is simply that he prefers to attach himself to some acknowledged diamond who is unattainable because she is already married. Which, you will admit, is quite another pair of shoes."

Perhaps it was because she was not expecting very much that Anna found Sir Aubrey perfectly charming. At Lady Holroyd's direction he took her in to dinner, and very correctly divided his attention between her and his other neighbour. But when he *did* turn to her, his conversation was very entertaining, and even when he was apparently engrossed in a tedious account of a very dull play that the other lady had recently attended, he managed to attend to Anna's needs in an unobtrusive fashion that was very comfortable, since *her* other neighbour was not only hard of hearing but was plainly much more interested in his own dinner than in doing the polite to a lady, be she never so attractive.

When the gentlemen joined the ladies in the drawing room, Sir Aubrey made no bones about his pleasure in her company, coming straight to her side and keeping her amused with his apt comments on a number of mutual acquaintances. He was not malicious, though he had a knack of light-hearted caricature that had her chuckling more than once. He paid her one or two compliments, and although she was no longer so naive as to believe them to be sincerely meant, he did it so beautifully that she was left with the feeling that they stemmed from genuine liking and approval.

Sir Aubrey was a skilled practitioner, but this impression was not wholly unjustified. He was inclined to be very pleased with young

Lady Wellasford. Indeed, he was almost prepared to believe that she would *do*. While not a classical beauty, her looks were striking, her figure was delightful and she had excellent style. Moreover Caro Holroyd had given him to understand that the Wellasford marriage was purely one of convenience, so the lady's husband was unlikely to make trouble. Not that there would be anything to make trouble about. Sir Aubrey's attachments were conducted with the utmost discretion and were surface affairs that never outlasted one Season. He would as soon have thought of wearing an outmoded wig or last year's waistcoat as of paying his attentions to last year's flirt. It was his custom to select some charming and popular young matron and use all his savoir-faire to win her favour in the face of all contenders. It was a sport at which he excelled. And as Margaret had shrewdly noted, he *preferred* married ladies. He could not then be accused of arousing expectations that he had no thought of fulfilling. He decided to invite Lady Wellasford to drive in the Park with him on the following day. That would give him a chance to assess her quality without committing him too far.

He had, alas, made one serious miscalculation. Julian, while outwardly perfectly affable, had not cared for the way in which Drysdale had singled out his wife. At so small and intimate a party he should have bestowed his attentions more evenly. It was bad form, to say the least of it. Julian, who had been amused and secretly flattered by the adoring gambols of Anna's youthful admirers, had decided at once that Sir Aubrey was a little too much of a good thing. If he was not actually a rake or a man of the town, he was a good ten or twelve years older than the innocent Anna, and infinitely more experienced. But though Julian might be the merest novice in the art of managing the female sex, he had, during his military career, learned a good deal about the handling of headstrong youngsters. To criticise Sir Aubrey at this stage of the game would, he felt, be a strategic error, perfectly calculated to set up all his wife's prickles, the more so since she seemed to be pleasantly impressed with the mountebank. So he allowed him to be a very pleasant sort of fellow, assured Anna that in winning his admiration she might now consider herself to be socially top-of-the-trees, and regretted that he personally had enjoyed so little opportunity of furthering his acquaintance with the gentleman.

He was a little startled to discover in himself a distinct sensation of disappointment, even annoyance, when Anna mentioned her engagement to drive with Sir Aubrey. It so chanced that this was the first occasion on which any one had usurped his privilege in this respect. The members of Anna's juvenile court were mostly unable to afford the dashing vehicles and the blood horses that were essential if one wished to invite a lady to drive in the park. Especially when the lady's husband drove such fine cattle. Thus Julian had come insensibly to count upon this hour as his, the more so since further riding lessons had long been found unnecessary. Anna had become a reasonably competent whip, but when they were in Town she still preferred to be driven. There was so much to see, so many friends to be acknowledged that one could not enjoy the exercise of a skill so recently acquired. She reserved that enjoyment for the occasions when they paid a brief visit to Wellasford, or sometimes, if there were few people about, at Richmond. Julian, driving with absent-minded ease, was able to talk to his wife almost as though they were alone—for one did not count the groom perched up behind—even though they were frequently interrupted by the exchange of greeting with a growing circle of acquaintances. He had not realised how much he had come to value these brief intervals of easy camaraderie.

During the days that followed, as the Season worked up to its peak and, gradually, the first deserters began to leave Town, Julian came to detest Sir Aubrey with a bitterness that he had not dreamed he could nourish. The damned fellow was always under foot. If he was not riding with Anna or driving her down to Kew to visit the Botanic Gardens, he was advising her, quite unnecessarily, thought her husband savagely, as to schemes for decorating the reception rooms at Wellasford (which he had never seen) or endeavouring to persuade her to remove to Brighthelmstone for the months of July and August, assuring her that *his* influence would be perfectly adequate to the task of hiring a genteel lodging, even at this late date. As for evening engagements, Julian thought *he* might as well have stayed at home. Within ten minutes of their arrival his wife was inevitably whisked away from him, and if he *did* chance to set eyes on her again before their carriage was called, she was, equally inevitably, in the company of Sir Aubrey. Reluctantly he was obliged to concede some admiration for the man's finesse, for there was never a word or an action to which a husband could take exception; never, even, a degree of attention so marked that it might give rise to a breath of scandal. The 'ton' placidly accepted the fact that young Lady Wellasford was Sir Aubrey's latest flirt. The only sufferers were the Wellasfords.

Anna suffered a degree of remorse for permitting Sir Aubrey to devote so much of his time and attention to her. She credited him with a good deal more heart than he possessed and hoped, anxiously, that he had not developed a genuine tendre for her. She did not really think so, because on the rare occasions when they were alone together his manner became distinctly formal. But conscience did not acquit her of using him for her own purposes. She liked him very well though she was not in the least in love with him, but it had seemed to her possible that the attentions of so notable a beau might have a desirable effect upon a laggard husband. After all—you might exact a promise of freedom to try your wings unfettered by conjugal responsibilities, but when you have achieved success beyond your wildest dreams, surely it behoved your husband to show some awareness of your success. Could he be impervious to the charms that had subjugated the lions of London? Perhaps Sir Aubrey's attentions would sting him into action.

The unfortunate Julian was torn between his determination to honour his promise to his wife and a strong desire to plant the ubiquitous Sir Aubrey a facer. Trouble was that the fellow never gave him quite sufficient cause to relieve his feelings in this way and he was, in any case, restrained by the knowledge that such behaviour must surely provoke a resounding scandal. Would it serve, he wondered, to attempt to distract his wife by setting up a flirt of his own? To be sure he had promised that he would not make her a laughing stock by blatant indulgence of what they had euphemistically described as his baser instincts. But flirting was different. His wife was in no position to cavil at that! And there was Caro Holroyd, ready to hand and, as she had shown with increasing frankness, perfectly willing to oblige.

Compared with Sir Aubrey he made a poor fist of it. His compliments lacked polish, his bearing was embarrassed rather than devoted. Most disastrous of all he lacked Sir Aubrey's subtle skill in disengaging from the most delightful dalliance if it showed signs of becoming inconveniently intense. Where Sir Aubrey would have pointed out a fine burst of country or a delightful pastoral scene, Julian found himself tenderly pressing the lady's hand, even kissing her fingers, and, on one disastrous occasion, her cheek.

No gentleman could openly blame the lady for that occurrence. Nor, at the time, was he in any mood to offer explanations.

He had planned to drive to Pittsfield House to give an eye to various improvements that were in progress, and had invited his wife to go with him. An invitation that she declined in favour of a long-standing engagement to attend a military review in Hyde Park. When he had ventured to press his claim, she had pointed out that the long drive into Surrey would make her very late for Lady Penmarston's theatre party which she was promised to attend that evening. This was perfectly true, and he would probably have suggested another day for the proposed visit to Pittsfield House, had it not emerged that her escort to the review would be none other than Sir Aubrey. If she preferred that gentleman's society to her husband's, not to mention the dust and noise and crowds of Hyde Park to a comfortable drive into the country, there was obviously no more to be said. Julian retired behind his newspaper with dignity—and with no idea of how close his wife had come to wavering at the sight of his dissapointed face. If only he had said, "Oh—let the fellow go hang. We could steal a day together, just the two of us," or something of that sort, she would have met him more than half way. But he did not speak again until he had finished his coffee, when he said coolly, "In that case I may not see you again today. I doubt if I shall be back before you leave for the theatre, so I had best bid you goodnight."

In such circumstances there was nothing a girl could do except feign a gaiety and an enjoyment that she was far from feeling. So much, at least, she owed her escort.

Julian, however, usurped the feminine prerogative of changing his mind. Just as he was about to set off, a groom arrived from Wellasford with a note from his father-in-law. That gentleman would appreciate the favour of a few words with him. The matter was personal and private, and he did not, at this stage, wish to take his daughter into his confidence. Could Julian find time, during the next sennight, to ride out to Wellasford so that they could have a quiet talk together?

A word with the groom eliciting the information that Mr. Morley was to be found at home, it seemed to Julian that there was no time like the present. If Anna was not to know of the business he would be obliged to devise some excuse for the visit, and of late he had come to rate his capacity for invention pretty low. Whereas today his excuses were already made. He had little heart any way for a solitary expedition into Surrey. He sent a message to the stables and shortly thereafter took the Watford road instead of driving south.

Eleven

Mr. Morley was delighted by Julian's prompt response but appeared to be in no hurry to explain the reason for his summons. In fact he carried his son-in-law off to the stables to inspect a beautiful mare that he had just bought, obviously a lady's mount. Julian rather naturally assumed that the animal was designed primarily for Anna's use, and enquired with a hint of mischief if it was trained to accept a side-saddle.

For the first time in their acquaintance Mr. Morley actually looked embarrassed, muttered something disjointed about Anna's progress in riding and hurried his companion out of the stable, although they had not nearly done justice to the mare's perfections. As they emerged into the yard he ran a finger round a stock that he seemed to find uncomfortably tight and said on an explosive sigh, "That's the nub of the matter, lad. That's what I wanted to see you about. The mare's not for Anna."

There was a brief silence, amazed on Julian's part but apparently restorative so far as Mr. Morley was concerned, for it was in an almost jovial voice that he continued, "It's an odd sort of thing to be telling one's son-in-law—all the wrong way round—and indeed I'm sometimes not certain whether I'm on my head or my heels. Fact is, I'm going to be married."

If Julian had been amazed before, this piece of information took him completely aback. He stared at Mr. Morley as though doubting the evidence of his ears. Fortunately this attitude seemed to please and amuse the older man, who, now that his secret was out, reverted to a much more normal manner.

"Not very observant, are you, m'boy?" he said cheerfully. "Though I suppose that's natural enough since you've only got eyes for that girl of mine. And very pleased I am to see it. We made up a grand match when we agreed together that you and Anna should wed, though I'll admit I never dreamed that I'd be the next to enter parson's mouse-trap. A bachelor all these years and thought to die one."

He lapsed into silence, pondering this incredible change of heart. Julian, who had recovered his powers of speech if not his composure, stammered as awkwardly as any schoolboy, "But sir, who is the lady?"

Mr. Morley chuckled. "Told you you wasn't very observant, didn't I? Just goes to show. I suppose you thought I was for ever dropping in at Portman Square for the pleasure of *your* company—or even because I was lonesome and missing Anna. And I'll not deny there was something of that nature in the beginning. I suppose it really started the day of Anna's presentation. That was the first time we really talked together, Margaret and me. Yes," he nodded happily, in response to Julian's exclamation of delight, "it's Margaret who has done me the honour of giving me her promise. I don't know where I found the impudence to ask her, a lady born as she was, and so rare and fine a woman. I suppose it got so there was no bearing it, wondering if there was just a chance that she might say yes, and thinking that by not speaking out I

175

was wasting days and weeks of happiness when maybe I'd not so many left to me. And do you know what she said to me? When I plucked up heart at last? She said, 'I was beginning to think that you were never going to ask me; that somehow I'd have to do it myself.' There's a woman for you! As sound and sweet as a pippin and straightforward with it. None of your die-away airs and graces like that silly Holroyd creature."

Julian expressed his very real delight and satisfaction in the news, declaring that it was the neatest possible scheme for keeping Margaret in the family. "And we are both much attached to her, you know. You could not have presented us with a more acceptable stepmama. Anna will be over the moon."

"You think so?" said Mr. Morley eagerly. "That would be splendid. Because Margaret has consented to marry me as soon as it can be arranged, but only if Anna can dispense with her services. I told you this was a topsy-turvy affair. I need my daughter's consent—or at least connivance—to hasten my marriage plans."

"Then you can safely arrange for the banns to be called without further loss of time," assured Julian confidently. "Anna will be just as delighted as I am."

Mr. Morley looked gratified. "I reckoned as much," he admitted, "seeing the three of you so comfortable together. And my marrying makes no difference to *you*, lad," he added simply. "Marrying so late in life, it's unlikely we'll be blessed with childer. But even if we should be so blessed, it won't affect Wellasford. I mean to make that over to you and Anna before I marry. I've enough from other sources to provide comfortably for Margaret."

For the last time Julian attempted to persuade Anna's father to sell him Wellasford. It was a half-hearted attempt, because he knew from the outset that it was unlikely to succeed. And even the temptation of being able to lavish the purchase price on extravagant gifts for his bride failed to move Mr. Morley. "Margaret would be the first to comb my hair for me if I behaved so scaly," he pronounced finally. There was a good-humoured twinkle in his eye, but his determination was never in doubt. He convoyed his son-in-law back to the house and his hospitality was as generous as ever, but he made no effort to delay Julian's departure.

"I leave it to you to be my emissary to Anna," was his valediction. "Just you put it to her that it's time she was done with junketing about Town. Once she settles down at

Wellasford she'll not need Margaret in attendance, and we can get married right away."

The injunction gave Julian rather seriously to think. He was fully in sympathy with Mr. Morley's views, but could not help feeling that he could scarcely put them to Anna in quite so forthright a fashion. Nevertheless it was in a mood of delighted anticipation that he maintained a brisk pace on the homeward journey, eager to share his surprising news with his wife.

His cheerful spirits were sadly dashed by the information, conveyed upon his arrival by Bailey, that Lady Wellasford was not yet returned from the Review and that Lady Holroyd was awaiting his arrival in the library.

Bailey had no great opinion of this visitor, but since she appeared to be on terms of intimate friendship with his employers he was careful to treat her with the greatest respect. She had arrived some half an hour earlier, enquiring first for Lady Wellasford (of whose present whereabouts she was perfectly well informed) and, when Bailey told her that both Lord Wellasford and his wife were from home she had calmly announced that she would wait a little while in the hope that one or other of them would return. Her business, she added airily, was important. Bailey knew what *he* thought of such encroaching manners, but was too well trained to show it, offering her ladyship refreshment, which she declined, and then showing her into the library.

It was her good fortune that Julian should return before his wife, but once assured of his identity by the sound of his voice speaking to Bailey in the hall, she made haste to set her scene to the best advantage. Taking a rose from a great silver bowl that stood on a low table she snapped off the head lest the wet stem soil her delicate gown and cradled it between her palms, holding it lovingly against her cheek and feigning an admirable start of surprise when Julian addressed her.

"Oh! How you startled me," she complained sweetly. "I had not heard you come in—or I would not have permitted myself to be caught stealing one of your roses." She held up the ill-treated bud. "It was so perfect that I could not resist. With me, you must know, it is not so much the colour or the scent as the exquisite velvety texture. I *must* touch." She brushed the rose lightly against her cheek and held it to her lips. What man could desire a better opening for a charming compliment? Lady Holroyd could think of several, and waited hopefully to see which would occur to her rather slow-topped admirer. Unfortunately Julian was wholly preoccupied at the moment with the news that he was eager to impart to his wife. He said civilly that there were plenty of roses and that he would ask Bailey to desire the garden boy to pick some for her.

The lady would dearly have liked to slap him for such oafishness. With truly admirable self control she said gently that she would not put him to so much trouble and turned instead to the ostensible reason for her call. Even this she could not approach in a straightforward way—possibly because it was a complete fabrication—but must needs apologise for trespass, urging prettily that only their long friendship had nerved her to such presumption. The thing was that she had received an enquiry from a prospective tenant, and would be grateful if Julian would let her know as soon as possible whether he proposed to renew the lease.

"For naturally you must have the preference," she finished, with a smile of languishing sweetness.

This, too, was wasted, for Julian's thoughts turned at once to the effect that Mr. Morley's impending marriage was likely to have on his domestic arrangements. If Anna had had her fill of Town life, they could retire peacefully to Wellasford. He for one would be heartily thankful to be rid of the Portman Square house and its saccharine owner, but it must be for Anna to decide. So much had been implicit in his promise. He assured Lady Holroyd that he would discuss the matter with his wife and would certainly let her know as soon as possible.

It was not a very promising opening for a tender love passage, but Lady Holroyd was skilled in the making of bricks without straw. She drew a deep, quivering sigh and announced that she envied him greatly. To his surprised and startled expression she enlarged pensively. "So fortunate! Two of you to confer together, to make decisions, to support each other. It makes my own loneliness seem more bleak by contrast. Do you wonder that I envy you?"

Julian felt more embarrassment than sympathy. He said bracingly that he was sure that Johnnie must be a tower of strength to his sister. "And only think how many friends you have," he went on, "any one of whom would be only too happy to be of service to you."

But this well-meant suggestion appeared

to plunge the disconsolate widow into deeper gloom. "Friends?" she repeated sorrowfully. "When even the oldest among them cannot remember my birthday?" And her pretty lips quivered and tears seemed imminent.

The threat of tears temporarily confused Julian's wits, or he might have recalled the fact that the lady's birthday was in the spring, even if he did not remember the precise date. As it was, he assumed—as she had intended—that the auspicious day was today. He embarked upon a lame apology for his forgetfulness, and as this effected no noticeable diminution in her woe, took her hand in his and, bending down, bestowed a comforting kiss upon her cheek.

This was a mistake. She turned to him, casting herself upon his chest so that he was obliged to put his arms about her, and assuring him mistily that she had known all along that she could perfectly rely upon him. At which inconvenient moment his wife, followed by Sir Aubrey Drysdale, walked into the library.

The speed with which Julian removed his encircling arms should have done much to convince both ladies of his total lack of enthusiasm for the position. He was, in fact, very annoyed. It was bad enough to be caught

A Marriage Arranged

in such a compromising position, but he could have explained it easily enough to Anna, who was always reasonable. But why must she bring Sir Aubrey into it? Hadn't she seen enough of the wretched fellow, spending the whole afternoon in his company, that she had to bring him home as well?

Sir Aubrey, who had not seen the kiss, though he had a fair notion that they had walked in upon as pretty a piece of flirtation as ever he had come across, was the first to recover his savoir-faire, with the heroine of the charming piece a close second. Anna, who had been aware of a sudden bleak desolation at the sight of Caro Holroyd in her husband's arms, murmured a mechanical greeting.

"Lady Holroyd called to enquire about the renewal of the lease," explained Julian, with a composure that sounded unnatural even in his own ears. "She has had an enquiry from a prospective tenant. I have said that we will let her know as soon as we have had an opportunity of discussing it."

Anna nodded non-committally and launched into an animated account of the impressive scenes of the afternoon. Neither visitor lingered unduly. Sir Aubrey preferred to win his plaudits on a wider stage. Lady Holroyd was well content that she had given that odious little upstart something to think about. Queening it at Almack's and bosom bows with Lady Penmarston, was she? Not to mention making mocking remarks about older females who tinted their hair. Well—that should teach her the folly of crossing swords with Caroline Holroyd. She only hoped that Sir Aubrey had seen enough to appreciate the pretty play to the full.

Left to themselves the married pair eyed each other warily, Julian wondering just how much his wife had seen and anxious not to commit himself too far, Anna emerging from her first sick shock to a much more healthy anger.

She said evenly, "Don't waste time teasing yourself as to whether I saw you kiss her. I did. I must beg that in future you will refrain from doing so under my own roof. Or do you regard it as hers? Talk of renewing the lease, indeed! Pretty talk! May I remind you, milord, that when I pledged you my troth, you undertook to refrain from such indulgence in amatory dalliance as must make me a laughing stock."

That was not exactly how Julian recalled the business, but this was no time to stand upon points. Military instinct urged that in this case counter attack was the best form of defence. He said savagely, "And do you mean to tell me that Sir Aubrey has never claimed the privilege of kissing your cheek? And you, my dear, are not a widow."

"Nor yet a wife," she retorted swiftly, before she realised where such answer led her.

There was a tense little silence. Then chivalry won the day. Julian said slowly, "I beg your pardon, Anna. I was wrong to taunt you so. And I beg that you will forgive me. It was—no—not wrong, but silly, to kiss Caro. Which is very much worse. But without sounding the most complete coxcomb I can't really explain how it came about. And I promise you sincerely that I had very much rather kiss you."

But that was going very much too fast in her present mood and she warded him off swiftly, exclaiming that she must hurry or she would be late for her theatre party. But he thought there was a warmer look in her eye and counted himself forgiven, spending a happy hour in planning what they would do when they surrendered the lease of this house and with it their ridiculous pretence of marriage.

Twelve

Anna partook of breakfast in bed next day. Not only had she been late home after her theatre party, having gone on to enjoy supper at the Bath Hotel with a group of friends (including Sir Aubrey Drysdale) but she had not quite decided on the proper attitude for an outraged wife to adopt towards an offending and slightly impenitent husband. To be sure Julian had apologised—but he had not seemed to take the business very seriously. That remark about preferring to kiss *her,* for instance. He had never shown the slightest inclination to do so. For the matter of that, neither had Sir Aubrey, though this she did not propose to tell her husband.

She let her coffee go cold while she pondered the various ways in which one might subjugate a husband who showed no disposition to join one's court, even when so notable a beau as Sir Aubrey had shown the way, and ended by wondering dismally if there was some essentially feminine quality lacking in herself, since none of her admirers showed any disposition to succumb to their much vaunted passions. She certainly did not wish to be 'mauled and kissed' as she phrased it by any over-bold aspirant to her favours, but here she was, nearly five and twenty, fêted, courted and admired—but unkissed. It was a depressing thought. And if she meekly submitted herself to the matrimonial yoke as she had agreed to do now that her brief butterfly hour was nearly done—well no doubt Julian would kiss and caress her in a dutiful sort of way, because he was kind and, she thought, quite fond of her. When first she had agreed to marry him that was all that she had expected, or indeed wished. But now she faced the fact that she wanted a good deal more than that. The truth was out in the open at last. Certainly since the day when he had driven her from Wayney's to Pittsfield House—possibly from their very first meeting when he had been so tactful and understanding about her antiquated dress, she had been learning to love him.

She had watched his dealings with his friends, with persons of rank and distinction, with his servants; and in all of them she had found food for glowing pride. Papa both liked and respected him—and that was indeed a compliment. And when she looked back at the weeks of her marriage she realised how completely she had relied on his support. He had left her free to choose her own path but he had always been close at hand. Even in the early days she had never felt shy or awkward because Julian was there and would certainly come to her rescue if she found herself at a loss.

She saw how, inevitably, she had compared all the other gentlemen she met with her ever-growing knowledge of Julian, and realised at last why she had felt only a detached friendliness towards even the most attractive and attentive. All unknowing, she had *grown* into love with her husband.

But the placid intimacy founded on mutual respect and forbearance that she had thought of as making an ideal marriage was no longer sufficient. She gave a twisted little grimace as she recalled that conversation with Julian about marriage. She had spoken quite frankly

of her willingness to bear his children. Well—
she was still perfectly willing. Even eager,
she admitted to herself, blushing furiously at
the mere thought, all alone in the big bed.

But it was not the possible heirs of Wellasford who concerned her at the moment. It was
Julian whom she loved and desired. And what
she wanted was not a temperate, lukewarm
loving but a fierce possessive passion. She
wanted him to catch her to his heart and kiss
her because he was driven to do so, and in
defiance of promises and foolish masculine
notions of honourable behaviour. And for the
first time she realised how strong a barrier
she had erected between them when she rejected wifehood. A barrier that he would not
cross and that pride forbade her to lower.

But the day must be got through, whatever
her private problems. She sighed briefly,
pushed aside the neglected tray, and had just
stretched out her hand to ring for Cicely
when a brisk tap on the door startled her.
Before she could reply the door opened a little
way and Julian's voice, crisp with impatience,
enquired if its owner might enter.

It was the first time that he had ever
requested this privilege, and although she
knew that it was almost certainly some matter
of urgency that had brought him to her door,

her heart-beats quickened and she could not resist a swift glance in the mirror to ensure that she was reasonably presentable before she called to him to come in.

It was a little annoying at first to discover that he did not appear to set any particular store by the unusual encounter, seating himself on the end of the bed without ceremony and apparently quite oblivious of yesterday's tiff. "Such news!" he exclaimed. "I wanted to tell you last night, but Randy kept me over-late and I thought you would be asleep when I came home. And then Margaret tells me that you were late home, too, and were break-fasting in bed. I simply couldn't wait any longer—especially with Margaret sitting there behaving so demure and unconscious. I must have laughed out loud. It was a dashed close-run thing, especially when she asked me if I had found Mr. Morley in good health. Good health! He had shed ten years! But of course, I had forgot that you did not know of my visit to Wellasford yesterday."

He then took pity on his wife's bewildered face and poured out the story with reasonable coherence. In her interest and pleasure she quite forgot to be self-conscious. She also forgot that she had indulged her taste for rich and delicate fabrics to the full when choosing her night robes, rejecting the modest cambrics and nainsooks of her girlhood completely. The one she was wearing at the moment was of apricot tinted silk mousseline, so fine that even with its matching wrapper it scarcely veiled the beautifully moulded arms and the proud curve of her breasts. And if his wife, in her excitement, was unaware of the enticing picture that she presented, her husband was not. He got up rather abruptly, and walked over to the window, gazing down into the street in an absent-minded sort of way as he summed up, "So you are all for an early wedding, as I am myself. Do you really need Margaret's further attendance? I should have thought that with the Season so near its end, you could probably manage without her, however much we shall both miss her society."

His wife concurring enthusiastically, he went on, "Then what answer do you wish me to return to Lady Holroyd? About the tenancy. Shall we let it go? We can perfectly well go back to Wellasford—I told you what your father had arranged about that—or we could go down to Pittsfield House. Though that would not be very comfortable at present with only half the alterations completed and hordes of workmen swarming everywhere. I'm sorry that I haven't devoted more time to the search for a suitable Town house, but if you wish it I am perfectly willing to renew the lease on this one. You will scarcely want to go to all the trouble of refurbishing yet another hired house, and from the point of view of accommodation I doubt if we could do better."

Anna hesitated, finger to lip. However uncomfortable, Pittsfield House would at least permit them to be virtually alone together. Surely, then, they would be able to find a way out of the web that they themselves had woven. And nothing would persuade her to renew the lease on Lady Holroyd's house.

Julian watched her, fighting back a fierce urge to take her in his arms, delectable as she was in her airy draperies, and kiss her so comprehensively that she would have no breath left for protest. And quite suddenly the hard-held control of the long weeks snapped. He did not give way to his impulse, since honour forbade. Instead he said silkily, "Of course it will make things very difficult for your gallant cicisbeo if we remove into the country. A shockingly long drive for the poor fellow, but I daresay his devotion will be equal to it."

The shock of this unexpected attack was considerable, the more so for its sharp contrast with the happy plans that they had been discussing so pleasantly two minutes previously. Anna was normally both equable and tolerant, but her own miserable musings had left her particularly sensitive to criticism. She, in her turn, flared up into open temper.

"And you, I suppose, will plead an engagement at one of your several clubs when you wish to visit your languishing lady-love."

She wished the words unspoken even as they were uttered, but it was too late. Julian's shocked expression told her so. He said uneasily. "You do not imagine—you cannot seriously believe"—and turned and strode out of the room without further debate, leaving the whole business of their future plans—indeed of their future—hanging in the air.

Anna buried her face in the crook of one elbow. She did not weep, but never had she felt so miserable. Of *course* she did not think that there was anything serious between Julian and Lady Holroyd, any more than there was a genuine attachment between herself and Sir Aubrey, but sauce for the goose—

She forced herself to lie still until the quivering of her mouth and the ominous pricking behind her eyelids abated. What was to do now? And as so often in her childish griefs, the answer presented itself swiftly. She would go home to Papa—take counsel of him. A visit of congratulation was his due in any case. A little ingenuity, and surely she could turn the talk to her own affairs.

Margaret, apprised of this plan, made some small demur. Had Anna forgotten that she was engaged to drive out to Kew with Sir Aubrey? Why not delay the visit to Wellasford until next day, when Margaret would be free to accompany her? But Anna, having once decided upon a course of action that promised some relief for her uncertainties, was not to be persuaded. She would go to Wellasford today. If Sir Aubrey chose to stand upon his rights, he could take her to Wellasford instead of to Kew.

"And what will you do with him when you get there?" demanded Margaret pertinently. "You cannot be private with your Papa and leave poor Sir Aubrey to his own devices. Don't tell me he can occupy himself with a book. I daresay he has never opened one since he left Eton—unless it was a Peerage and Baronetage—and that, I strongly suspect, he has by heart."

But Anna, usually so reasonable, would have none of it. "Then he may ride beside the carriage," she said pettishly, "and when he has rested the horse and refreshed himself, he can take himself off wherever he wishes."

Margaret wisely abandoned the argument, saying only that it was a pity that this was the one day that she had begged off in order to visit her former mother-in-law, with a view of advising her of her impending re-marriage, and that therefore she could not offer to make one of the party and take the entertainment of Sir Aubrey off Anna's hands.

"And a fine chance I should have of being private with Papa if *you* were with me," chuckled Anna, good humour restored now that she had won her way.

Sir Aubrey's carriage eventually set out for Wellasford with its owner driving. Lady Wellasford seated beside him, and his head groom perched up behind, Sir Aubrey, ap-prised by a brief note of his goddess's change of plans, heroically declaring that he per-fectly understood Lady Wellasford's desire to be private with her Papa, and adding that he would be quite happy to stroll about the grounds—which he understood to be well worthy of a visit—until such time as she was ready to return to Town.

Anna's other plans went less smoothly. Papa was delighted to see her and to have her felicitations upon his proposed marriage at first hand, but he was far too preoccupied with his own affairs to be fully sensitive to the difficulties of hers. When she casually broached the question of her future domicile, he sounded positively astringent.

"Surely that is for your husband to decide," he pronounced severely. "I cannot imagine that any man of sense would choose to live an idle, fashionable existence in Town unless he was obliged to do so. As a bride it was natural that he should indulge you with a taste of fashionable gaiety, but what is there in the existence of your Town beau to satisfy a man of energy and intelligence? You will need a Town house, of course. Your husband will find it very useful for business purposes. Mighty convenient for the City and the Docks, since I understand that he plans to extend his Uncle's Indian business interests. And you, no doubt, will like to spend a week or so in the great metropolis from time to time. But I cannot imagine Julian wishing to make his permanent home anywhere else but here. Indeed, if he is thinking of disposing of Pittsfield House I might make him an offer for it—or he might consider a long lease. But that is looking very far ahead. As for you, my dear, it is time you settled down to running your husband's home and filling his nursery.

That is plain speaking, but it has been in my mind for some time, seeing the way the gentlemen flock about you. Don't want you getting your head turned by these fashionable ways of going on, for I'm willing to lay you any sum you choose to name that not one of them means the tenth of what he says."

Since Anna had already come to the same conclusion she returned a soothing answer, assuring him that she was not in the least taken in by the flattery that was heaped upon her and that she was very willing to give up the delights of the social whirl and settle down in the country, but he was not yet done with her.

"That's as may be. And while we're on the subject, I don't care to see you spending so much of your time with that Bartholomew baby that drove you down today. No better than a windsucker—all show and no performance. Though maybe there I'm blaming you without cause. It's for your husband to put his foot down on such behaviour as must make you the talk of the town. I'll have a crow to pluck with him the next time I see him. So just you mind to behave more seemly and see you get back home well before the darkening. Married woman or not, I don't hold with such goings on."

A Marriage Arranged

The moment did not seem opportune for a discussion of difficulties of which this irascible parent was blissfully unaware. Anna meekly prepared to rejoin her escort, and although Mr. Morley's sense of hospitality insisted that he offer the gentleman a glass of wine before he faced the rigours of the return journey, he did not encourage them to linger. Nor was Sir Aubrey, who had spent a remarkably boring afternoon wholly deprived of any kind of audience, at all inclined to outstay his welcome. He set out at a spanking pace, his spirits rising with every turn of the wheels that carried him nearer to his chosen milieu. One paid lip service to the delights of country living, of course. It was the proper attitude to take so naturally Sir Aubrey observed it. But a careful observer might have noticed that his actual sojourns in rural surroundings were brief and widely spaced. He was delighted to put this one behind him. It was a pity, however, that he allowed his relief to beguile him into abandoning the main highway and taking a side road out of Broxbourne, promising his charge that he would show her some charming bursts of country and quite forgetting that other road users might be less skilled than he.

Thirteen

It was inevitable that the accident should happen on the loneliest stretch of road that they had encountered all day. A lumbering family chariot, fortunately unoccupied, was partly at fault, taking a bend so wide that it was impossible for Sir Aubrey to avoid it entirely. He was able to rein his horses aside, so that they suffered no injury, but the light carriage, in consequence, swung across the path of the oncoming chariot, and since both vehicles were travelling at speed, the impact was considerable. Most of the glass in Sir Aubrey's carriage was shattered, and unfortunately several of the flying splinters pierced

Anna's thin silken sleeve, inflicting several deep scratches and, in one or two cases penetrating more deeply and causing considerable bleeding.

Sir Aubrey and his groom sprang down and hurried to examine the pair of blood greys that had been wrenched to so abrupt a halt, Sir Aubrey cursing with a vigour and invention that caused the groom to bestow an admiring glance upon him.

It was left to the driver of the chariot to attend to the lady who eventually managed to fumble her way out of the carriage and to descend in rather wavering fashion into the road, her right hand clutching her left arm, whence a steady trickle of blood descended to bespatter the dusty road. His driving might have been negligent but his head was screwed on the right way. Moreover he put the needs of the injured lady even before the claims of the sturdy pair that were poled up to the chariot. They were not, of course, *his* horses. He supported her to the side of the lane and obliged her to be seated on the rising bank that bordered it, ripped up the sleeve from the wounded arm to bare the injuries, carefully removed a visible sliver of glass, causing the blood to well more freely, and twisted a strip torn from the ruined sleeve above the punctured wound to slow the bleeding.

"Thank you," faltered Anna, rather breathlessly. "You are very kind."

"Never you fret yourself for that, miss," returned the coachman heartily. "That was a nasty shock you got, and some of it my blame I'm fearing. Just you bide quiet until you catch your breath. The bleeding's about stopped," he added in satisfied tones.

At this point Sir Aubrey joined them.

"What the devil do you mean by it?" he demanded furiously. "You were all over the road. No thanks to you that my greys are not ruined, obliging me to pull them up in such brutal fashion."

It was plain that the coachman did not care for these strictures. He flushed to his ears, a dull angry red, and his mouth took a stubborn twist. But he was at a double disadvantage, both as a servant addressing a member of the wealthy and leisured class, and because he knew himself to be at least in part to blame for the accident.

"And downright sorry I am, sir," he returned "and as thankful as you are yourself that they've come to no harm, such beauties as they are. Reckon I took the corner too wide and too fast—as I've already said to miss, here. But you was coming pretty fast your-self, sir," he ended sturdily.

Sir Aubrey snorted at this perfectly justifi-able rebuke. "Impudent lout," he exploded furiously. "If you were *my* servant you would pay dear for this blundering."

"Then it's just as well I'm not, ain't it?" remarked the coachman placidly. "My own master'll give me a right trimming when he sees the state his paint work's in. If he's in bad skin he'll maybe stop the damage out of my wages. But at least he wouldn't stand here in the road rating me for what's over and done while there was a lady in sore case that needed to be taken to a 'pothecary as soon as maybe." With which he turned on his heel, knuckled an eyebrow at Anna with a respectful smile, and addressed his attention to his own affairs.

Thus rudely reminded of his responsibili-ties, Sir Aubrey enquired awkwardly as to Anna's well-being. The groom went off to address soothing remarks to the fretting horses—and to hide a contented grin at the way in which the stranger had set Sir Aubrey to rights. Anna, shocked and shaken by the accident, answered as composedly as she could, though her voice was not quite steady as she declared that she did not think that the services of a physician were necessary but admitted that she would be glad to lie down for a while as she had a bad headache, and that she thought that perhaps a cup of tea would have a beneficial effect.

Consultation with his groom assured Sir Aubrey that there was a small inn just this side of Turnford—no more than two miles away—where these comforts could probably be found. The sufferer was tenderly assisted to climb back into the carriage—an undertaking which caused her head to swim in the most horrid fashion—and Sir Aubrey rather unwillingly resigned his horses to the skill of the groom, feeling it incumbent upon him to sit beside the lady and tender moral support, though he very much hoped that no other variety would be required of him.

He had by this time assimilated all the awkwardness of the situation. He devoutly hoped that the inn that his groom had mentioned would prove to be a respectable place, for he had formed the intention of bestowing the lady there in the care of the landlady. He himself must repair to Town without loss of time. Any other course must be disastrous for both of them. Let it but be whispered that they had been benighted together, and the lady's reputation must be irretrievably lost, his own fair name sadly tarnished. It took him no more than five minutes to convince himself that whatever her injuries and need of masculine support, Lady Wellasford's true interests would best be served by his own prompt departure.

His hopes were sadly dashed by the appearance of the inn. It was no more than a village ale-house, and sadly dilapidated as regards paint and plaster. The landlord, when repeated assaults on the tap-room door eventually summoned him from whatever occupation had been absorbing his attention, seemed to be amiable but stupid. He was not a prepossessing figure, his breeches unlaced, his shirt open to the waist, the whole emitting a strong odour of mingled sweat and beer with powerful overtones of the poultry house. Sir Aubrey had to repeat his story twice before full appreciation dawned, with all its accompaniment of enjoyable horror and sympathy.

Fortunately for both Anna's comfort and Sir Aubrey's conscience, the man's wife proved to be a good deal cleaner than her husband and reasonably brisk and efficient. They had no accommodation for travellers, but Miss—Sir Aubrey had thought it as well to make no mention of Lady Wellasford's name—could lie down in her daughter's room. Her daughter had been married only a month ago, which was a fortunate circumstance since they had only the two bedrooms. She sallied out energetically to welcome this romantic guest, but upon setting eyes on Anna's wan face and ominously stained dress, promptly exclaimed that she could not take the responsibility of caring for the young lady unless a physician was summoned to attend her. There was a very good one, a Doctor Underwood, in Turnford. Any one would tell them where he was to be found.

Reluctantly—since every extra person admitted into the incident increased the danger of scandal—Sir Aubrey sent his groom in quest of this useful personage. Nothing less would satisfy Mrs. Burton.

That good lady was, however, able to provide Anna with an excellent cup of tea, which brought a little colour back to her cheeks. Having drunk it she was able to essay the steep stairs that led to the tiny bedchamber without feeling that she might turn giddy, but she was nevertheless very thankful to be able to lie down and close her eyes.

The groom presently returned with the news that the doctor would be with them in half an hour or so. Sir Aubrey mulled this over carefully and then announced his decision to

continue his interrupted journey to Town
without further delay. Mrs. Burton drew a
deep breath to tell him what she thought of
such a heartless proceeding, but he forestalled
her. "It is essential that I inform her ladyship's relatives of her mishap without loss of
time," he explained, choosing his words with
care. He placed a roll of bills on the table.
"Perhaps you would be so good as to discharge the doctor's fee in my behalf," he said.
"For the rest—it is some small recompense
for the trouble to which you have been put."

Mrs. Burton, divided between excitement
at the discovery that her guest was a real live
ladyship and a swift calculation of the size of
the roll and its possible value, allowed him to
make good his escape without enquiring as to
how soon she might expect his return.

Sir Aubrey hesitated for some time over
his next difficult decision. Should he call on
Lord Wellasford in person, or would a note
suffice to inform him of his wife's whereabouts? By the time he reached Town he had
decided that a personal call was the proper
thing. Wellasford was bound to appreciate
the delicacy of the position and the care that
he had taken for the preservation of her
ladyship's good name. He would naturally
want to express his gratitude and it was only

decent to afford him the opportunity of doing so. A call in Portman Square, on top of the delay caused by the accident, would make him late for his dinner engagement, but noblesse oblige, he reminded himself, and set out forthwith, trusting that at this hour he could be certain of finding Lord Wellasford at home.

In this hope he proved to be justified. In every other aspect of the brief interview that followed, he found himself utterly confounded.

"You mean to tell me that you actually left her alone, with some unknown female of humble origins, and without even waiting until the doctor had seen her?" There was scarce-controlled fury in Julian's voice, but Sir Aubrey, cocooned in the knowledge of his own superiority in all matters of ton, did not recognise the danger signals.

"But my dear fellow," he drawled, at his most urbane. "You must see that it was the only thing to be done. I don't know who the doctor was, but so close to Wellasford it is perfectly possible that he would recognise your wife. He might even have recognised me. And the discovery of the two of us, apparently keeping a rendezvous at a quiet inn, must have given him the oddest notion of our relationship. I am sure the last thing that either of us desires is any hint of scandal."

"You are mistaken," returned Julian levelly. "The last thing that *I* desire is to think of my wife injured and alone, and possibly in incompetent hands. As for scandal—*I* would never believe a word against her, and neither she nor I would care a fig for what the world might say."

Such plain speaking discomfited Sir Aubrey. He shrugged. "A high flight indeed," he yawned, the epitome of sophisticated boredom. "You are singularly fortunate."

"So, for the moment, are you," retorted Julian, grim-faced, "because my most urgent preoccupation is to reach my wife as soon as it may be achieved. Once I am assured of her well-being, my friends will wait upon you."

At last he had succeeded in startling the self-satisfied beau. "Pray don't be so absurd," he exclaimed, in a much more vigorous voice. "Here have I been at the utmost pains to protect Lady Wellasford's reputation—as I have just explained to you. You can have no possible reason for calling me out."

"No?" queried Julian, icily polite. "Well I have pleasure in telling you, sir, that it's my belief that it was not my wife's reputation that concerned you, but your own. Such a non-pareil of perfection as you are—such a Galahad—no breath of reproach must stain your noble name. I take leave to tell you that you are a cold-hearted, conscienceless coward. *Now* will you fight me?"

"If you insist—yes," snapped Sir Aubrey, stung at last. "Though nothing could be better calculated to provoke just the scandal that I have been at such pains to prevent."

That was true. Whatever his private fury, his burning desire to work off his frustration on the man who was in some part responsible for it, there could be no denying that a duel, whatever the cause agreed by the protagonists, invariably left unpleasant smears of suspicion and scandal on a number of possibly innocent parties. Julian had a sudden horrid vision of the face of Mr. Morley as some one told him of his daughter's disgrace.

"Very well," he conceded reluctantly. "But," brightening, "there is no reason why we should not have it out here and now, with our fists." That would be best of all, he thought contentedly, and awaited Sir Aubrey's agreement.

Sir Aubrey was one who preferred words to blows. He eyed his antagonist, who was already beginning to struggle out of his coat, with distaste, and at the back of his mind was the thought that he would have something to say to Caro Holroyd when next they met. A marriage of convenience, indeed! Well, it was proving deuced inconvenient for *him*!

"Certainly," he said with some dignity. "If you feel that it will do any good to batter me to a pulp—and to have everyone enquiring how I came by my injuries. With the small sword, if report speaks truth, you would probably be my master. With pistols—and without modesty—you would be a dead man. But I have never favoured what is so ludicrously described as 'the manly art'. Manly it may be. Art it is not. Now *you*, I understand, have actually been commended by the great Jackson himself. If, however, you wish to engage in a contest where there is no doubt of your emerging the victor, behold me, quite willing."

Whatever his other attributes, there was no doubt that he was Julian's master with *words*. That poor fellow was reduced to suggesting that his exasperating opponent leave the house and make no undue haste about returning to it. This did at least clear the way for his own departure in search of his wife. When his temper had cooled a little he acknowledged that this was much more important than a temporary and slightly shameful satisfaction.

Fourteen

"Though I'd have something to say to *my* husband if he went off and left me with strangers, and me so sadly out of kilter," concluded Mrs. Burton, straightening the quilt and beginning to put away Anna's clothes. "I'd best wash this petticoat for you, ma'am—milady, I *should* say—and I'll try soaking the dress in cold water though I doubt if the stains'll come out. Let's hope that husband of yours'll have the sense to bring you some clothes when he comes back, though Doctor Underwood did say that you was to stop in your bed until he called again tomorrow."

The doctor's visit and the examination and

dressing of her arm had left Anna too limp to make much conversational effort. She had simply permitted Mrs. Burton's flood of chatter to wash over her soothingly. But this could not be allowed to pass.

"But Sir Aubrey is not my husband," she corrected.

"Not your husband?" exclaimed Mrs. Burton, her eyes rounding in surprise.

"No. Just the gentleman who was driving me back to Town after a visit to my father," explained Anna, hoping wearily that this sounded sufficiently respectable. "He will have gone to tell my husband about the accident."

"Then no doubt we can expect his lordship here in a fine pelter," decided Mrs. Burton. "Though where he's to sleep is more than I can think. There's no room for him here. P'haps he'll drive on to Turnford once he's satisfied himself that you've taken no serious harm."

"I daresay he will. That is, if he comes at all." Then, seeing the good soul's shocked expression, she hastily added, "Sir Aubrey may not be able to find him, you know, until it is too late to set out. I do not really look for him until tomorrow."

"Then you may as well settle yourself down

and try to catch a little nap," pronounced Mrs. Burton, draping the stained garments over her arm and picking up the bowl of water that the doctor had used for his task. "I'll bring you up a morsel of chicken and some apple tart for your supper. It's not just what you'd call invalid fare but I daresay you'll take no hurt from it. Doctor Underwood said you wasn't feverish."

She clumped awkwardly down the stairs with her burden, meditating the while on the strange ways of the Quality. Who ever heard of a husband not setting out immediately when he heard that his wife had met with an accident? Especially when there was no question of expense to stop him, and his wife was young and bonny. Not long married, neither. Mrs. Burton, having finally noticed that her guest wore a wedding ring, had also marked that it was still shiny-new. She shook her head sadly over such heartless behaviour.

Her opinion of the Quality was to rise considerably when she met 'her young lady's' husband. He arrived some two hours later, driving himself in a curricle, the exhausted state of the horses testifying to the speed he had made. He waited only to discover that he had found the right place, cast a swift, assessing look at its style, and bade the groom see to the horses himself and, if the stabling was not to his liking, take them on easily into Turnford as soon as they were rested.

"I shall not need you again tonight," he finished curtly, and a rather indignant Mrs. Burton who had overheard this exchange, wondered where he thought he, or the groom, were to sleep.

He rose a little in her estimation when he turned to her with a pleasant smile and asked her name, saying that he understood he was indebted to her for giving shelter and care to his wife in her need.

"The name's Burton, sir. Milord, I mean. And I did no more than my duty. But your wife's a gentle, pretty creature that makes duty a pleasure. You'll be thankful to know that Doctor Underwood found little amiss with her beyond the shaking up and the loss of blood. A day or two in bed will set her to rights, he reckons, nor he doesn't think she'll be scarred. I've just brought her supper tray down and she's eaten most all of it so you can go up and see her right away. The door on the left at the top of the stairs."

The gentleman did not immediately avail himself of this permission. He said simply, "I cannot thank you enough," and put out his hand. Mrs. Burton hesitated for a moment, then awkwardly rubbed her own hand on the skirt of her dress and put it into his. She expected him to shake it with becoming gratitude but was completely stunned when he raised it to his lips and gently kissed it.

She found herself staring at her hand as though it had suddenly undergone a magical transformation. When she was again capable of speech she muttered shyly. "Sir, you shouldn't have gone for to do that. Me skin's all rough and not overly clean."

Whereupon his lordship smiled down at her in the kindest way, as she later told her awed spouse, and said, "Your hands were good enough to tend my wife, and that is more than good enough for me."

The voice that bade him enter when he tapped on the door of Anna's room was heavy with weariness. He walked in quietly and said gently, "My poor dear!"

Anna who had been drooping against her pillows wishing that she had something to read to distract her miserable thoughts from a throbbing arm and an unsatisfactory husband, sprang erect with a jerk that made her head begin to throb too. For a long moment the two stared at each other.

Julian saw a wife very different from the delightful vision on which he had turned his back only that morning. In a plain white linen nightgown borrowed from the landlady, high to the neck and long-sleeved, her lovely hair carefully brushed and braided by those workworn hands, she looked like a little girl. There were dark shadows under her eyes and her cheeks were pale. But as she saw the look of tender adoration writ plain on his face, colour began to steal into hers. Unconsciously she clasped her hands to her bosom as though to calm her quickened breathing.

Julian came forward quietly enough and sat down on the side of the bed, just as he had done this morning, but now held out his hands and Anna put hers trustfully into them.

"I don't know whether to hug you for relief that you are still alive or to scold you for tumbling into such a scrape when I was not at hand to get you out of it," he said thoughtfully. "But first I think, this."

He let go her hands and, with due care for the injured arm put both of his about her and drew her close. She made no attempt at resistance but yielded herself to his hold and held up her face like a child for his kiss. It began gently enough, for it was indeed a kiss of thankfulness that she was alive and safe. But her innocent response and the warmth and sweetness of her in his arms so went to his head that it very soon developed into a kiss of a very different kind. Indeed kisses, for there were those lovely smooth eyelids to be caressed and the curve of cheek and chin to be outlined with gentle lips before he came again to that warm responsive mouth.

"And you may thank heaven for Mrs. Burton's nightgown," he told her, smiling, his first longing assuaged. "It *is* hers, I take it? Very proper and modest, too. If it were not for that, I might forget all about your wounded arm and your need for rest and quiet. If it were that confection that you were wearing this morning, now, I really could not be answerable for the consequences." And smiled to see her colour rise.

But Anna was already recovering her poise. "It was very kind of Mrs. Burton to lend it to me," she said defensively. "And it is beautifully white and smells of lavender." She giggled suddenly. "I don't think she meant to be funny. She told me in such a solemn voice that it was her laying out gown." And then, at his puzzled face, "*I* didn't understand, either. It's her shroud. She had it all ready, beautifully laundered and put away for when she dies. To be laid out in. But she also meant that it was her very best. She said her everyday ones weren't good enough. She is the kindest creature."

"Yes. And I can quite see that it is just the sort of gown that one *would* choose when one had finally renounced the world and the flesh. But I have not. Very definitely. So you will understand my preference for your yellow nonsense—if you call it yellow. But now my love, you really must rest. Remember that, a very long time ago, I promised to cherish you, and now, thank the Lord, I am free to begin doing so."

"Yes, that is all very well, and I look forward to the fulfilment of the rest of those promises," returned the invalid, mischief gleaming in her lovely eyes. "But meanwhile, where are you going to sleep tonight?"

"Here," announced her husband calmly. "You don't imagine that *I* am going to shab off like your other beau? I'm sure Mrs. Burton will be able to find a chair or a truckle bed or something in which I shall do well enough."

He quelled her protests in the most convenient—and delightful—way, and then drew away from her to smile a little. "Do you know," he said quizzically, "I have just realised that I ought really to be grateful to the ineffable Sir Aubrey? If it were not for his services today, it might still have been weeks before we came about. As it is, my dear and only love (this with an admonishing little shake), will you now surrender your freedom? Will you be in very truth my wife?"

And Anna, her cheek against his shoulder, answered by holding up her face for his kiss.

Let COVENTRY Give You
A Little Old-Fashioned Romance

GREAT ADVENTURES IN READING